SECRETS

OF

SILVERGROVE

Books by Mitchell R. White

Brannigan Mysteries

Secrets of Silvergrove

Forget-Me-Nots and Forgotten Graves

Blue Iris, Blood Morning

Lotus, Lilies, and Last Courses (Summer 2026)

Roses are Red, Violets are Murder (Fall 2026)

Summers Rose Investigations

End in a Dead Heat

So Easy It's Criminal

Tacos, Sunsets, and Murder

The Drowned Duck (Summer 2026)

Murder with Incidental Music (Winter 2026)

Writing as M. R. "Doc" White, Ph.D.

Samarqand: Prelude

Samarqand

Redeeming Lost Pegasus (Fall 2026)

Lost and Fallen (Winter 2026)

Bloodwine Warriors Trilogy (2027)

Writing as Mitchell R. White, Ph.D.

The British Slang Handbook

SECRETS

OF

SILVERGROVE

MITCHELL R. WHITE

WHITE JADE BOOKS

SECRETS OF SILVERGROVE

Cover Art and Design by M R White
Interior Text Design by M R White
First Electronic Edition: March, 2025
First Paperback Edition: April, 2025

ISBN 979-8-9927943-0-4 Kindle Edition
ISBN 979-8-9927943-1-1 Paperback
ASIN B0DZ5N82ZN Kindle Edition
ASIN B0F32953JY Paperback

WHITE JADE
Publications, LLC

To the beauteous Paula Jo, who picks up the pieces when I break, who smiles when I tire, and who makes the journey worth traveling.

"Flowers are restful to look at. They
have neither emotions nor conflicts."
— Sigmund Freud

"When the world wearies and society fails
to satisfy, there is always the garden."
— Minnie Aumonier

"Coffee. Garden. Coffee. Does a good
morning need anything else?"
— Betsy Cañas Garmon

Table of Contents

Chapter One

Aileen Brannigan slurped her coffee, barely catching a splash before it stained her last clean work shirt. "Double drat!" she blurted, not wanting to ratchet up the invective too early in the day. She placed her travel mug on the counter, pulled off a clean paper towel and bent to clean up the mess.

The doorbell chimed, because of course it would when she was down on all fours.

"Oh, for heaven's sake," she mumbled, standing with the careful deliberation of someone whose joints had their own opinions about morning movement. She grimaced, hoping the ibuprofen bottle was still on her desk at work.

The doorbell pleaded again, insisting.

Aileen tossed the paper towel, missing the counter entirely. Another thing for later. She hurried to the front door, pulling it open to find Rick Malone's impossibly cheerful face.

"Morning, Missus B!" His grin was criminal at this hour. Aileen blinked, waiting for her brain to catch up. "You okay?" Rick asked, concern wrinkling his forehead beneath his blond crew cut.

"Fine, fine! Is it time already?" Aileen marveled. She'd never mastered early.

"I can grab the keys, get us opened up." Rick rolled his skateboard under his left foot, ready to ride. "You come along when you want." Rick pointed down. "There's something brown on your knee, Mrs. B."

Aileen sent a silent plea skyward as she swallowed another curse. "Thanks," she squeezed out. "Hold on." She stepped to the antique console in the entry and rummaged through a bowl of keys.

"Here," she said, "I'll be along soon. If that delivery guy from EastTex Plants gets there before me, just have him wait in his truck. He takes his coffee black."

Rick scooted off with a casual "Got it!" tossed over his shoulder. Aileen noted the small holes dotted across the back of his t-shirt, and his jeans looked like they'd been through the wars. She shook her head and closed the door, returning to her cooling coffee. A quick peek at the hall clock showed she was going to be late again. Third time this week. At least old Gran Janner wouldn't complain, she'd given all her clocks away years ago.

Aileen gathered up Gran's boxed meals, a small breakfast of cold cuts, crackers and cheese, plus a lunch to nuke. She wished she had more time, better meal prep skills; her Adopt a Granny charge deserved better. Aileen pursed her lips and pushed away her guilt. No, it was this or nothing. She balanced her travel mug on top of the boxes, pushed her new puzzle book into her handbag, and scooped up her car keys. She'd worry about her abandoned corn flakes later.

The early April morning had the cool freshness that promised steamy humidity later. Aileen wished for a light jacket but wouldn't backtrack now. She pulled her front door closed without locking. This was Silvergrove, not Chicago.

She nearly dumped everything on the driveway trying to unlock her old Chevy one-handed. Haste makes waste, as she knew Gran would chide. She set the meals onto the passenger seat, then started the car. The coffee stain on her knee caught her eye. She pinched a used tissue from the center console and attacked the mess. Her aging Chevy needed a good scrub-down. Someday, she promised as she put the car in gear.

The drive to Gran Janner's took minutes in the familiar Silvergrove quiet, early on Saturday. She caught the light at Highway 21 green for the day's first miracle. Her long list of tasks waiting at the garden center slid by behind her eyes. She swerved around the stubborn brown tabby planted in the middle of Pine Street. Same cat, same spot, almost every time.

Gran Janner was chatty this morning, of course. Weather, hummingbirds (Aileen topped off the feeder), the neighbors. Why was she never this talkative when Aileen had time? Behind her smile, Aileen listened carefully, giving gentle responses. The old woman's loneliness nearly broke her heart. She waited as long as she could before interrupting Gran to ask if she needed anything else, and then excused herself with as much grace as she could muster.

Back through the light at the highway, green again, and Aileen could hope to beat the delivery man to Brannigan's Bloomers. Perhaps karma was real, she pondered as she turned into her parking spot. Maybe it was...

The key stuck in Brannigan's Bloomers' front door lock. Again. He jiggled it twice, muttering about WD-40, then pushed through into darkness that smelled of potting soil and yesterday's marigolds. Rick stowed his skateboard behind the counter next to a lopsided stack of old puzzle books and considered the morning ahead.

The garden center lay quiet at a quarter to seven, except for the hum of grow lights in the greenhouse. Spring meant early starts, but Rick didn't mind. These peaceful moments before opening belonged to him alone.

He flicked on the main lights and headed for the break room, his footsteps echoing on the concrete floor. The ancient coffee maker needed coaxing, but soon it gurgled to life, promising blessed caffeine. While it brewed, Rick grabbed cleaning supplies and tackled the front displays. The morning air drifted in through the propped door as he worked, carrying the scent of an east Texas dawn, cool and damp.

Watering took forever, as it always did. Rick moved down the aisles with the hose sprayer, checking each hanging basket, each table of potted flowers. The rhythm calmed him down after the tense clash at home that morning. The peace lilies needed trimming. He added it to his mental list, right after 'reorganize the terra cotta pots' and 'check the fertilizer inventory.'

His phone buzzed in his pocket. Then buzzed again. And again.

Rick's jaw tightened as he pulled it out. Twelve texts from Verona, starting at 3 AM. The first few were casual enough: a simple hello, then a question about his work schedule, with hints about getting lunch, maybe at Noodle Phonatic. By 7 AM they'd turned desperate. The last one just said "please."

His thumbs hovered over the keys. Resentment built, sharp and final. He typed: Stop texting me. This isn't okay. But he'd been in school

3

with Verona for two years. The awkwardness would ripple through every hallway meeting, every meal, even at soccer practice. Better to let it fade. He erased his text without sending.

He shoved the phone back in his pocket and grabbed a flat of petunias with more gusto than necessary. He paused to roll his shoulders. Morning light strengthened as he arranged the blooms, pink and purple faces turning toward the sun. By the time he heard Aileen's car in the parking lot, he'd almost forgotten about the texts.

"Morning, Rick!" His boss bustled in, arms full of papers, handbag, fresh puzzle book, and her ever-present battered travel mug. "Sorry I was so scatterbrained when you came by. EastTex should be here any minute. Do you know if we have room in the back for —"

The rumble of a diesel engine cut her off. Through the braced door Rick could see the familiar green and white bobtail truck backing up toward the loading door, Jerry at the wheel, right on schedule.

"Already cleared space, ma'am," Rick said, reaching for his clipboard. "Coffee's fresh, too."

Aileen smiled. "What would I do without you?"

Rick grinned, shrugged and headed for the loading area through the break room, pouring a quick cuppa for Jerry. He could relax, here, when things got tough at home. The morning stretched ahead, full of soil and flowers and honest work. His phone buzzed again in his pocket. He didn't check it.

✧ ¤ ✧ ¤ ✧

Darwin glanced out his bedroom window at the morning shadows stretching across Silvergrove's familiar streets. His mom wouldn't be home for hours; that consulting visit to Texas Christian would be intense. And then the four hour drive home. Dad was still stuck in Seattle at some architect's conference. At almost thirteen, he was quite capable of taking care of himself. This gave him more time to work on his Go game.

His phone vibrated and he looked at his left screen. Text from Rick: **Thanks for the boost on that algebra problem**. Darwin typed **NP Glad I cd help**. He really liked that phone-to-computer relay script he'd written. He could keep going on his game without interruption.

The doorbell sounded once, twice. Darwin considered not answering. How could anybody know he was in? Probably just some sales guy. And this online game with the 6-dan master in Korea was intense. Darwin felt he had a chance, but he needed to focus.

The bell sounded again, then started going off every few seconds. He jumped up and ran to answer his door, annoyed that he'd been disturbed. He was about to clobber that Go master and he worried he'd never get his flow back.

The smiling faces of his two grandmothers, Bea Wheeler and Irene Henslee, greeted him. He changed his face from grumpy to pleased. Wouldn't do for these two to see him upset, though he wasn't sure why they'd come.

His long, silent pause caused Irene to ask, "Are you going to let us in?"

Darwin scooted back and made a stage-theater bow of welcome, sweeping his arm toward the foyer. The ladies laughed and entered, gifts in their arms. "For you, Darwin. An easter basket," Bea said. Irene handed Darwin a wrapped box. The women then put Darwin between them and escorted him to the parlor.

Night and day, Darwin mused. Chalk and cheese. Petite and bird-like Granma Bea, who didn't weigh much more than Darwin himself. And tall, stately Grandmother Irene, long hair flowing, always so formal in spite of herself. They had been his sporadic babysitters since before he could remember.

The one thing they had in common was academic achievement. Granma had two Ph.D. degrees, packaged up as a Doctor of Science in a special program. Grandmother "only" had one Ph.D., but she'd been visiting professor at a dozen universities around the world in her career. Math, computers, psychology. Darwin knew they also had a dozen other degrees and certificates between them.

Darwin loved them dearly. If they'd just lighten up with the teaching and testing, he thought. He didn't need that anymore, he was ready to find his own educational path. He didn't dare show any reluctance to their kind but firm structured tutoring, though. He felt lucky they visited only a few times a year now.

"Great to see you," Darwin said without much energy. "What brings you here?"

Bea chimed in, speaking for both the women. As usual. "Irene has a longer spring break than usual, and I finished my master lectures at Cal Poly a week early. We got to talking and, well," she trailed off, shrugging.

Grandmother Irene spoke into the gap: "I've got this new test for learning speed I really need your help with," she said. "We thought, since we left off last time with exploring quantum chromodynamics, that we'd proceed further with that while I checked your learning rate."

Darwin sighed. Trapped by his own extreme interest in quantum physics. He wanted more, as he wanted to study physics at Cambridge University in England in a couple of years. He just knew he'd get in. Imagine studying where Crick and Watson cracked DNA, where Hawking defined black holes, and Newton got hit by an apple. He could barely contain himself.

"Okay, but first some milk and cookies. Then we can give your challenge a go."

The ladies headed to the kitchen in Darwin's wake. At least he got extra cookies when the grandmothers visited.

✧ ¤ ✧ ¤ ✧

The bell above the entrance sounded its plaintive chime as the door opened, sending a shaft of April morning sunshine across the weathered concrete floors. The kind of sunshine that made Texas feel like heaven on earth: warm enough to kiss your shoulders, but not hot enough to send you running for shade. Aileen looked up from her labeling, breathing in the mix of potting soil and sweet alyssum that always reminded her why she'd chosen this life.

Charity Hofflich drifted in like a lost butterfly, trailing the scent of spring with her. The bluebonnets and Indian paintbrush had exploded along County Road 23 this year like God himself had gone crazy with a paintbrush. Lord help her, that woman could kill a cactus with nothing but good intentions.

"Aileen!" Charity's voice carried across the front greenhouse. "I need your expert help. Again." She twisted her hands together, a habit that showed up whenever she faced decisions more complex than choosing breakfast cereal.

"Coming, coming." Aileen set down her label gun and wiped her hands on her apron. The morning was too perfect to rush. Last week's church bazaar had worn everyone out, but in the best way possible. They'd raised enough money to fix the fellowship hall roof, and Miss Eleanor's strawberry pies had sold out faster than teenage gossip could spread. Before she reached Charity the door chimed again, and in walked Ephron Dewitt, looking every bit the retired farmer in his worn overalls and Kubota cap. Aileen wasn't one to borrow trouble, but these two together in her shop? She didn't think it would come to blows, but it was early yet.

"Morning, ladies," he nodded, heading straight for the perennials. "Church gardens need some sprucing up before Easter. Especially after all those kids trampled through them during the bazaar's egg hunt." His tone was gruff, but Aileen caught the smile lurking under his complaint. Those same kids had bought him out of his famous honey-roasted peanuts, after all.

Charity latched onto Aileen's arm. "Everything I planted last month died. Everything! I think my soil is cursed."

"Soil's not cursed," Ephron muttered, loud enough to carry. "Just needs proper care and attention." He paused to look out of the greenhouse windows, where redbud trees were showing off their purple blooms against a sky so blue it hurt your eyes to look at it too long.

Aileen shot him a look that could endanger small caterpillars. "Now Charity, let's start with something simple. What kind of sunlight does your front bed get?"

"Um... the morning kind? Or maybe it's afternoon." Charity's forehead wrinkled. "The sun definitely hits it. Sometimes. When it's not too cloudy."

Aileen thought Ephron's snort could've been heard in Dallas.

A breeze carried the sound of wind chimes from Miss Betty's porch next door, mixing with the chirp of cardinals and the distant rumble of Mr. Peterson's garden tractor turning over spring soil. The weather had been showing off lately, as if trying to make up for last year's drought. The pecan trees were leafing out and mockingbirds were building nests in everyone's crepe myrtles.

"What about these?" Aileen pointed to some marigolds. "They're pretty hardy —"

7

"Oh, but yellow clashes so with my shutters," Charity fretted. "And those," she pointed to some petunias, "remind me of my great-aunt Mabel's curtains. She had terrible taste."

Rick, restocking shelves nearby, stepped in with the timing of a guardian angel. Last Saturday he'd been the hero of the bazaar too, rescuing the face-painting booth when little Jimmy Wilson had decided to give himself tiger stripes with a permanent marker. "Ms. Hofflich, have you considered peonies? They're gorgeous, smell amazing, and they're practically indestructible."

"Really?" Charity perked up. "Indestructible sounds perfect!"

"And these begonias," Rick continued, gesturing to a display of pink blooms. "They're like the Toyota of flowers. Reliable, low-maintenance, and they look good without trying too hard."

While Rick guided Charity through her horticultural crisis, Ephron sidled up to Aileen. "That boy's worth his weight in gold," he whispered. "Now, about the church garden..."

"Yes, let's talk about plants that people actually know how to care for," Aileen said, leading him toward the shade-loving varieties. "Speaking of church, when's the next potluck? Patricia's got a new banana pudding recipe she's dying to show off."

"Second Sunday," Ephron said. "Though if it's anything like her last 'experimental' dish, maybe she should stop experimenting. Is she still running the food pantry?"

"I'll pretend I didn't hear that. Yes, she's got the food bank well in hand. When she's not working the mortuary." Aileen helped him select an armful of coral bells and bleeding hearts. "These will look nice along the prayer garden path."

Ephron huffed out a gush of air. "I don't see how anybody can countenance Patricia Gaillardo running a food bank out the back of her father's mortuary. Rest his soul." He lifted a flat of hostas. "Gotta have some green. At least the funeral business is slow."

Aileen saw Rick at the register, ringing up Charity's purchases: three peony plants and a small flat of begonias that might survive the season. She watched Rick gather up the flowers and move outside, arranging the plants in Charity's back seat as if he were loading precious cargo. That kid was a real find, Aileen thought. Too bad about his home situation.

Ephron appeared at her elbow with his church garden selections. "Need a hand getting these in my truck? And just add them to my tab."

"Lead the way," Aileen said, gathering up pots. "And yes, I'll tell Patricia to stick to traditional banana pudding."

The morning sun had burned away the last of the dew as they loaded the plants, and somewhere in the distance, a mockingbird was singing. Just another spring day at Brannigan's Bloomers, where good gardens began and miracles occasionally happened, even for Charity Hofflich.

Chapter Two

Aileen's feet ached after ten hours of hauling mulch bags and dealing with indecisive customers. The thought of cooking made her want to cry.

"I deserve a meal out," she muttered to her steering wheel. But where? Casa Sol Vineyard's prices would give her wallet heartburn. Besides, she didn't feel like wine, and she knew the waiter would press. Sombrero Roja? Her stomach twinged at the memory of their five-alarm enchiladas, and those were the tame ones. She was about to turn down Camellia Street to home when the Classy Cook Café's neon sign caught her eye. Perfect; simple comfort food was exactly what she needed.

The electronic door chime greeted her as she walked in. Before she could spot an empty booth, a familiar voice called out.

"Ms. Brannigan! Join us!" Fagan Sertsma's fresh, carrot-topped face grinned at her from a corner booth. Andy Burrell, the middle school principal of more than a decade, lifted his water glass in greeting. Aileen hesitated. She'd been looking forward to a quiet evening, but declining might cause an awkward scene.

"Thanks," she said, sliding into the vinyl seat beside Fagan. Cathy brought over a menu, but Aileen waved it away and ordered the diner's famous chicken sandwich and sweet tea. The fellows barely acknowledged her arrival before diving back into their debate.

"The dock's rotting, Fagan." Andy jabbed his fork in the air for emphasis, a flake of grilled salmon balanced precariously on its tines. "You can see it from a hundred yards away! Hell, I bet you could spot it from space."

The rich, smoky aroma of the fish wafted across the table, making Aileen's mouth water. The salmon's cedar-planked perfection, glazed with what looked like maple and soy, made her regret playing it safe.

11

Next time, she promised herself, watching Andy savor another bite. Next time, no playing it safe.

"The budget won't stretch, Andy. Unless you want to raise property taxes?" Aileen noticed that he hadn't eaten much, skipping the mixed veggies, and he was stirring the roast juices around on his plate, clockwise and back.

Aileen's order appeared over her shoulder and she tucked in with more appetite than she'd expected. She watched the men volley arguments back and forth, their voices rising and falling like they were smashing shots on a tennis court. Aileen ate, her focus on each bite, letting their words wash over her.

"Aileen," Fagan said, "you're a sensible person. What do you think about the City Lake situation?"

She swallowed her last bite of wedge fries. "Honestly? The city underfunds all its green spaces. The garden club's been trying to get new planters for the walking path for three years." She pushed her plate away. "And I should really head home —"

"Say, do you fish?" Andy interrupted, leaning forward. "The bass are really biting this time of year. They're hungry after the cold winter we had."

"I —"

"You ought to come out this weekend," Fagan jumped in. "I've got an extra rod."

"Well —"

"The morning bite is best, but evening works too —"

"Have you ever tried fly fishing?"

Their enthusiasm pinged between them like a pinball, leaving Aileen no room to wedge in a response. She felt like she'd just fallen off of an old-style merry-go-'round.

"Who's ready for dessert?" Cathy's voice cut through the fishing frenzy. The café owner appeared tableside, order pad in hand, her green eyes sparkling. "We've got fresh apple pie, just came out of the oven."

"A la mode for me," both men said together. "Cathy, you keep on cooking like this," Andy said, "you may have to marry me."

"What, and disappoint half of Silvergrove?" Cathy smiled as she turned and walked away with an exaggerated hip sway.

"Man," was all Andy could muster. Fagan shook his head.

"I should really get going," Aileen said, seizing her chance. "Early day tomorrow." A white lie among friends, who'd notice?

At the register, with the guys distracted by their pie, she leaned close to Cathy. "Thanks for the rescue."

Cathy winked. "I know that trapped look when I see it. Get some rest, honey."

Cathy handed across all the change, and Aileen handed her back a dollar. All she felt she could afford, after splurging on dinner out. Cathy smiled and pocketed the tip, waving goodbye as Aileen turned to the door. Cathy's gracious understanding of how tough it could be on a woman business owner made Aileen glad she'd stopped in.

The spring night raised goosebumps on Aileen's bare arms as she took a deep breath of the crisp air. Her dinner hadn't been the quiet affair she'd planned, but at least she hadn't had to cook. Sometimes, she thought as she walked to her car, that was victory enough.

Aileen's old wooden back porch creaked under her weight as she settled into a weathered Adirondack chair, a chipped mug of coffee warming her hands. The Granmama's Bakery pastries from yesterday's delivery sat untouched on a paper plate, remnants from the garden center's Saturday rush that were too stale to give away and too good to waste. Spring in Texas had found its footing, the morning air carrying that particular sweetness that meant rain was coming, Monday afternoon or night, she supposed. She dove into the last few puzzles of her new volume, regretting that these magazines lasted so few days.

She watched a male cardinal flit between the branches of her overgrown crepe myrtle, its red feathers bright against the pale morning sky. The past week had been brutal at Brannigan's Bloomers. Two funeral arrangements, three last-minute wedding consultations, and the usual stream of regulars wanting advice about their withering houseplants. That was nothing compared to what lay ahead. Easter loomed just two weeks away, and in Silvergrove, Texas, that meant every front yard and business planter space would need its annual resurrection.

At this rate she'd never get her own yard refreshed. Cobbler's kids have no shoes, she brooded.

The coffee cooled as Aileen thought through her store inventory. She'd need at least twice the usual stock of Easter lilies, and probably more of those pastel petunias Mrs. Henderson always insisted were "just the thing" for the church entrance. The thought of church made her glance at the clock – 8:15. She could still make it to the early service if she hurried. After a quiet hour on her porch, Aileen chose to stay out in nature. She needed to move, though.

Aileen went inside and pulled on her old college sweatpants and the running shoes she'd bought three years ago, still looking almost new. This pretty morning deserved better than hymns and small talk in the church foyer.

The streets of Silvergrove were quiet as she started her speed-walk, most of the town's two thousand residents either still asleep or getting ready for services. Her pace was brisk at first, confident even, until the gentle slope leading to City Lake reminded her just how long it had been since she'd done any real exercise. Her breaths came in short puffs as she slowed to study the Bradford pears lining the path. They'd bloomed early this year, their white petals already carpeting the ground like unseasonable snow.

Aileen almost bumped into the Aspens as she turned onto Marigold Street. Terry and Rowan, on their way to church. Lovely couple with some odd ideas about raising kids, she mused as she regained her stride and pace. She wondered where Verona Aspen might be, as most Sundays they strolled to services together. Verona was turning out okay in spite of her rearing. She gave the girl no more thought as exercise forced her to focus.

The lake came into view, its surface rippling with a strengthening breeze. Andy's questions from last night about the park's condition echoed in her mind. He'd been right. The wooden dock listed to one side like a drunk trying to stand, its boards warped and splintering. The paddle boats, once a summer staple for local teenagers, sat upturned on the shore, their faded blue and yellow paint peeling to reveal patches of rust underneath.

14

The landscaping wasn't much better. Someone had planted pansies along the walking path, but they'd forgotten to account for the deer that treated City Lake Park like their personal salad bar. Half-eaten stems stuck up from the mulch like tiny surrender flags. The shrubs weren't faring much better. They needed a good feeding and mulching. All the dead limbs she saw in the larger trees disturbed her a bit.

When Aileen reached the cluster of benches at the south end, her legs shook. The morning's earlier brightness had given way to a welcome blanket of thin clouds, and she tilted her face up, letting the cool air dry the sweat on her neck. She'd rest here for a while and enjoy nature.

✧　✠　✧　✠　✧

Aileen's peaceful moment lasted exactly three minutes before voices invaded the park's quiet.

"Mrs. Brannigan!" The call came from Jessie Burnsides, her blonde ponytail bouncing as she jogged up with her friends in tow. Jessie's cheerfulness seemed immune to physical exertion, her smile as bright as it was during her shifts at Lendon's Full Service Fuel & Lube over on Highway 14.

Ryan Ruggle followed close behind, her long legs eating up the distance with elegant strides. She'd grown into her looks over the past year, all sharp cheekbones and olive skin that made her look more like a fashion model than a high school sophomore. Verona Aspen brought up the rear, her dark curly hair gathered in a messy bun, wearing the same Edson Keating High track team shirt Aileen had seen Rick wearing in the shop the week before. Rick wasn't big, but that shirt covered Verona's small frame like a collapsed hot air balloon. So that's where Verona is, Aileen thought. A good choice, out in nature on such a pretty morning. Maybe she'd make the late services at Second Baptist.

"Six miles today," Ryan announced, dropping onto the bench beside Aileen. "We're training for the half-marathon in Austin."

"I can barely manage this walking path anymore," Aileen admitted, rubbing her knees. "My running days are well behind me."

Jessie brightened. "You should meet Coach Chapin! He's seventy-three and still coaches with the Saturday morning group. He says age is just a number you use to make excuses."

15

Aileen waved off the suggestion, but her chest tightened. When had she started acting old, giving in? She was barely fifty, though some days her joints seemed to disagree.

"Doesn't Cheryl run with you all?"

"Not today," Verona chimed in. "She's off winning some skeet tournament."

"Ah" was all Aileen could get out, her breath still labored. She remembered the pretty immigrant from Armenia, now a citizen, and the girl's daunting reputation. Maybe the best shot in the region, the old guys at the coffee shop said.

The conversation shifted quickly, the way it always did with teenagers. One moment they were discussing training schedules, the next they were asking about Rick's plans for prom. Aileen noticed how Verona's fingers twisted in the hem of Rick's shirt at the mention of his name.

"What colors are you all wearing?" Aileen asked, steering the conversation toward safer ground. "I've been experimenting with some new ideas for corsages. Not the traditional roses and mums."

Ryan leaned forward, suddenly interested. "I'm wearing emerald green. What would go with that?"

For the next fifteen minutes, Aileen found herself sketching possibilities in the air with her hands. White orchids with trailing ivy for Ryan's green dress, pale pink garden roses with silver ribbon for Jessie's blush gown. She described delicate flower crowns that would put any traditional corsage to shame, mentally calculating costs and prep time even as she spoke. She floated the idea of the girls helping with assembly, for some cash and discounts. When Verona finally joined in, asking quietly about blue hydrangeas, Aileen pretended not to notice how red the girl's eyes had become.

"Break's over," Ryan announced, checking her watch. "We've still got three miles to go."

Aileen watched them disappear around the curve of the lake, ponytails swinging in unison as they chatted away, unaware of their effort. She should have brought her phone to note down all the flower combinations they'd discussed. The old ledger book she used at the shop was filled with Post-it notes and random scraps of paper, hardly an efficient system. Maybe it was time to let Rick show her how to use some of those planning apps he kept talking about. At least teach her a note app on her phone! She felt so prehistoric after her pleasant talk with the girls.

The thought of Rick brought back Verona's expression, and shame coiled in Aileen's stomach. She hadn't meant to hurt the girl by mentioning Rick's uncertainty about the prom. She'd only been thinking out loud, the way she often did with her customers. Sometimes she forgot that teenagers wore their hearts so close to the surface that casual words could cut deep.

She pushed herself up from the bench seat, her muscles protesting. The walk home seemed longer, each step jarring her knees as she tried to outpace her guilt. The morning church crowd was just leaving Second Baptist when she passed, and she raised a hand to return their waves, not slowing her stride when Mrs. Henderson called out something about Easter flowers.

Once home, Aileen meant to head straight for the shower, but her comfortable, old sofa beckoned. Just five minutes to catch her breath, she told herself, sinking into the cushions. The next thing she knew, sunlight was streaming through the living room windows at a completely different angle, and dried sweat tightened her skin.

She sat up slowly, her neck creaking in protest. The clock on the wall read 11:45. So much for her productive Sunday morning. As she moved to the shower, Aileen found herself thinking about Coach Chapin and the Saturday running group. Maybe next weekend, she thought. Maybe it was time to stop making excuses.

✧ ✩ ✧ ✩ ✧

The industrial fan at No Painz No Gainz whirred overhead as the girls changed in the locker room, its rhythmic swoosh competing with top-forty hits playing through tinny speakers. Verona caught her reflection in the mirror and rolled her eyes at the gym's graffiti-style logo painted on the wall behind her. The name was trying too hard to be edgy, but that was Silvergrove, always a few years behind the trends.

"Lunch at Casa Sol?" Ryan suggested, pulling a cream-colored jumper over her head. "My treat."

Jessie paused halfway through lacing her sneakers. "I don't know..." She wasn't comfortable with Ryan's offer to pay. Her dad Derek always said to "go Dutch" when out with friends, and her weekend paycheck from Lendon's was already earmarked to help with the family's monthly car insurance.

"Come on," Ryan pressed, her dark eyes sparkling. "Marcus works Sundays. You know, the one with the dimples?" She patted her designer handbag. "Besides, I'm good for it."

"We could invite Rick," Verona ventured, trying to sound casual as she braided her hair. "He sometimes helps with the wine deliveries on —"

"No." Ryan and Jessie answered together.

Verona's fingers fumbled in her braid. "I was just thinking —"

"We know what you were thinking," Ryan cut in, not unkindly. "Give it a rest."

"How can you afford Casa Sol anyway?" Verona switched targets, her voice sharp. "You don't even have a job."

Ryan's smile turned secretive. "Let's just say I have easy ways of making quick cash."

Verona opened her mouth to push further, but settled for a sullen "whatever." After a moment, she nodded. "Fine. I'll go. But no wine!" Ryan gave an exaggerated eyeroll while Jessie giggled.

The walk to Casa Sol stretched nearly three miles along the lakeshore, their muscles loose and cooling from the morning's run. Spring sunshine filtered through new leaves, dappling the path ahead. The conversation bounced between junior prom dates and next week's tests until Ryan groaned about her upcoming math exam.

"I'm totally gonna bomb it," she declared, kicking a pinecone off the path. "History too, probably."

"You're not worried?" Jessie asked, her ponytail swinging as she turned.

Ryan shrugged. "School's such a bore. Who needs it?"

"Some of us do," Jessie replied. "My parents will yank me from Lendon's if I drop below an A average."

"God, that creepy old man?" Verona wrinkled her nose. "I don't know how you work there."

"Mr. Lendon's not creepy," Jessie bristled. "He's actually nice. Pays above minimum wage, and I can adjust shift times whenever I need to study."

The conversation drifted to their encounter with Aileen that morning. "Her flower ideas were amazing," Verona sighed. "I wish I could work at Bloomers, help with the prom arrangements..."

"You just want to be near Rick," Ryan teased. "Besides, Jessie's got her job and I don't need the money."

Verona's retort died in her throat as a horn blast scattered them like startled quail. A ponderous Rolls Royce Phantom V swept around the corner, quicker than the girls could believe, its burgundy and cream paintwork gleaming in the sunlight. The horn tooted again, an absurd fox-hunting melody that seemed to mock their scramble for safety.

Ryan's middle finger shot up at the chauffeur, who acknowledged her with an elegant nod. In the back seat, Val Boucheron's wave transformed into a matching gesture when she recognized Ryan.

"Jesus on toast," Jessie breathed as they watched Trey, the impossibly handsome Italian chauffeur, guide the classic car into a perfect park. "That was close."

They reached the restaurant entrance just as Trey helped Val from the car. The woman shouldered past them into the foyer, muttering "Pearls before swine" loud enough to carry.

"Age before beauty," Verona mumbled at Val's retreating back.

Ryan gave a genuine laugh for the first time that morning. "Where'd you get that one?"

"Read your history," Verona said, lips pursed. "Winston Churchill, of course."

They watched helplessly as Val commandeered Ryan's favorite waiter Marcus and swept toward the wine bar like she owned the place. Another server, James, intercepted them and led them to a deck table, carefully positioned out of Val's sight.

Once seated, Verona and Jessie's commentary about the Boucheron family flowed like port from the vineyard's cellars.

"Why is Val like that?" Verona asked.

"Old man Boucheron's dying," Ryan reported, unfolding her napkin. "Dad says all that money can't save him now."

"I suppose that could make her that rude," Verona said.

"And wasn't there something sketchy about how his wife died?" Jessie added, warming to the gossip. "Ursula, right? Plus their son's always jetting off to God-knows-where. He just shows up when he needs cash."

Ryan studied her menu with unusual intensity, her only contribution a muttered, "They're not that bad."

She remained quiet through their shared appetizer of stuffed mushrooms, responding to further conversation with noncommittal hums. The meal flowed by; chicken here, fish there, and a small dessert for Ryan. Verona said she wasn't allowed that much sugar, and Jessie remained silent, not wanting to push the bill any higher. When the check arrived, Ryan pulled a sleek credit card out of her Pippin bag without looking at the total.

Their exit stroll took them past the bar where Val Boucheron held court like a disheveled queen, several empty glasses lined up before her. Jessie's steps slowed, her face flushing with remembered anger, but Ryan grabbed her arm while their waiter stepped between them and Val's tired stare.

Outside, the spring afternoon glittered warm and bright, the lake reflecting sun-sparkles as they started their walks home. Verona and Jessie split off first, still buzzing about their narrow escape from the Rolls. Ryan watched them go, her face still, before turning toward the private road that led to the Boucheron estate.

✧ ¤ ✧ ¤ ✧

Cheryl's arms ached. Nine hours of competition under the Texas spring sun had taken their toll, but here she was in the Open Finals at the Lufkin Skeet Championship. Not bad for someone who'd started the year in the Juniors.

The last pair of clay pigeons waited. She'd missed three all day; not terrible, but not perfect either. Her opponent, William, a weathered man with silver hair and steady hands, had just missed his second bird. If she could break both of hers...

20

She settled into position, feeling the weight of the Beretta Silver Pigeon across her arm. A late Christmas present from her parents, this gun was two inches longer than her usual one, and a little heavier. Still, at thirty inches it swiveled like a dream and the balance was superb.

Time for this new friend to earn its first trophy.

The first orange disc arced against the blue sky. Track, squeeze, break. One down.

Last bird. Last shot. Everything narrowed to the moment. "Pull!" The clay pigeon sailed. Her barrel followed, smooth as silk. The report echoed across the range, and the target shattered into dust.

Cheryl stood still, amazed by the last pieces settling to the ground. She knew she wasn't close enough to that disc to guarantee a hit. One pellet, maybe. She smiled. It didn't matter, she had won. She had won!

Applause broke out. Cheryl lowered her shotgun, allowing herself a smile as competitors rushed to congratulate her. First place in Open Division. The only teen among adult shooters. The trophy, her prize, gleamed in the late afternoon sun, golden brass and shiny silver on white oak. Someone pressed an envelope into her hands: the thousand-dollar prize.

Her father Alexander appeared beside her, taking the envelope without a word. He gave a single nod, the same one he'd give if she'd remembered to take out the trash. The other shooters' praise faded in her ears as she watched him tuck the check into his shirt pocket.

The drive back to Silvergrove stretched long and quiet. Cheryl watched East Texas pine trees blur past, her trophy lying forgotten in the back seat. She'd hoped, just maybe, this time would be different. That winning the Adult Division might finally get a real response from her dad.

"Tonight's advanced class starts at seven," Alexander broke the silence. "Master Sato is covering joint locks."

"Dad, I'm tired. Can I skip the dojo just this once?"

His knuckles whitened on the steering wheel. "You need to remember where we came from, Cheryl. Armenia was not kind to us. The government —" He paused, jaw working. "They would have killed us all if we hadn't been strong. Even changing our names might not save us here."

Cheryl sank lower in her seat. She'd heard this speech before, but it still made her stomach knot. She wondered if all the running, all the obsessed training, would ever be enough to outpace whatever shadows her father saw in the rearview mirror.

"I'll be ready for class," she said quietly, watching Silvergrove's familiar water tower appear on the horizon. Her father nodded, satisfied, unsmiling.

The trophy rattled on the back seat as they turned onto Cypress Street, the golden shooter on top tilted at a weary angle.

Chapter Three

The bell above Brannigan's Bloomers entry jangled as Aileen unlocked the front door, admitting the crisp Monday morning air and the scent of early spring. She flipped the sign to 'OPEN,' though she knew it would be at least an hour before any customers wandered in. Mondays were reliably slow, which made them perfect for catching up on paperwork.

The ancient coffee maker sputtered to life while Aileen settled at her desk, spreading out the jumble of receipts, sticky notes, and her weathered logbook. Two past-due items jumped out immediately: Mrs. Henderson's hanging baskets and old Mr. Pierce's tomato starts. She'd have to get those sorted before the pre-Easter rush hit.

"Rick's right," she muttered, fingering the dogeared corners of her logbook. "We need to computerize this mess." She grabbed the pad of orange Post-Its, the ones she reserved for important reminders, and scrawled 'AFTER EASTER – Computer System!!!' in bold letters. The note went straight onto the scratched screen of their point-of-sale terminal, where she couldn't possibly miss it. One more antique piece of equipment begging to be replaced.

The coffee maker finished its final gurgle when the shop's door burst open hard enough to rattle the wind chimes. Chief Roland Couch stood in the doorway, his wispy white hair catching the morning light, eyes darting around the shop like he expected trouble behind every potted plant.

"Chief?" Aileen's pulse spiked. "What's wrong?"

Couch looked at her as if she'd materialized out of thin air, then cleared his throat. "Mind if I look around, Aileen?" He took off without waiting for assent.

She hesitated, then nodded. "Let me just..." She grabbed the nearest tool, a sturdy rake, and followed him toward the break room. There she found him frozen, staring at the coffee pot like it held answers to life's unasked questions.

"Want a cup?" she offered, reaching for a clean mug. Aileen knew it was fifteen years since that night at the Big Rig Truck stop, when he'd encountered two truckers with short fuses and loaded weapons. He touched his missing earlobe as she poured. These days Roland Couch approached everything like it might explode.

"Thanks." He wrapped both hands around the mug, tension easing from his shoulders. "You seen any strange characters around lately?"

Aileen bit back a smile. "Other than gardeners, you mean?"

Their shared laughter seemed to break whatever remained of the morning's strain. Couch leaned against the counter, looking more like himself. "Got reports of someone wandering around town late last night. Male, probably thirtyish. Nothing concrete, just a lot of 'my cousin's neighbor saw' type stuff."

"Could it be one of the high school kids? They look older every year."

"Could be," he agreed, but his frown suggested otherwise. "Still, awful lot of calls this morning about it."

He insisted on finishing his inspection, but Aileen had already dismissed the matter from her mind, returning to her inventory of Easter stock. By the time Couch waved goodbye from his cruiser ten minutes later, she was deep in calculations about her EastTex Nursery order.

The bell chimed again, and Aileen looked up to find Andrew Burrell hovering just inside the door, looking as out of place as a cactus in a rose garden. Her first thought was that something must be wrong at the middle school if its principal was in her shop at this hour.

"Andy?" She set down her watering can. "Everything okay?"

He wandered the aisles like a lost soul, picking up and putting down items at random. His brown blazer was immaculate though not new, his light aqua shirt sported a passable starch job, and his bowtie was almost straight. His fingers drummed against a bag of potting soil, then fidgeted with a display of garden gloves.

"I was wondering," he started, then stopped. Cleared his throat. Started again. "The Dream Canvas is doing their dry run of 'Guys and Dolls' this Thursday evening. Before opening weekend?" His words tumbled out faster now. "I can get us in, and maybe. Well, dinner after? If you want?"

The teenage awkwardness of this middle-aged man's invitation caught Aileen off guard, in the best possible way. Her recent resolution to get out more made the answer easy.

"I'd love to," she said, watching relief soften the tension from his face. "I'll call Rick in to close the shop."

Andy nearly made it to the door before spinning back around. "Oh! Six o'clock? Can I pick you up at your place?"

"Perfect," she smiled, and he floated out to his car. She never did find out why he wasn't at school.

The rest of Monday unfolded with its usual rhythm. A few regulars picking up supplies, some phone calls about Easter arrangements, the quiet buzz of the grow lights in the greenhouse. Aileen even worked in a few puzzles over a relaxed lunch. By closing time at seven the spring twilight was settling in, painting long shadows across the parking lot.

Aileen locked up, her mind already on tomorrow's ordering tasks. She fumbled in her oversize handbag until she found her keys, and something made her pause. There, under Miss Betty's massive oak, a figure stood motionless in the deepening shade. Her hand lifted automatically in greeting, then froze mid-wave as Chief Couch's morning visit rushed back to her.

The figure didn't move. Didn't wave back. Just stood, watching.

Aileen's fingers fumbled with her car door. Once inside, she jabbed the lock button two, three times, her other hand already pulling up the police number on her phone. As she pulled out of the lot, she could still see him in her rearview mirror, a darker shadow among gloom, standing still beneath the ancient oak.

Twilight settled over the Boucheron estate like a silk shawl, softening the mansion's imposing French-inspired lines. Solar-powered pathway lights clicked on automatically, illuminating the long, tree-lined drive where ancient oaks stood sentinel. The place hadn't changed much in seven years, Ethan Riley thought, watching from the edge of the property. Still the same limestone and excess, still that air of old money gone to seed.

He counted the lit windows: fewer than before. The third floor was dark except for the corner suite where Marshall Boucheron lay dying. Second floor showed lights in what had been Ursula's rooms, now likely Val's domain. Ground floor blazed as usual, though the west wing, where the red jade cat had been displayed, remained dark.

Ethan remained motionless in his brushy hide as he surveyed the outbuildings. The old artist's studio, Ursula's pride and joy, appeared to have had no visitors in the years he was away. The windows were cloudy with grit and the roof looked unstable. The servant's quarters had several lights going, but nobody moved outside. With so few residents in the mausoleum, Ethan doubted they worked past six anymore.

Movement caught his eye: Trey Spalding, crossing from the garage to the main house, elegant as ever in his chauffeur's uniform. Some people aged; Trey got more polished. Even at this distance, Ethan could see how the courtyard lights caught the silver at his temples, adding to his distinguished appearance.

Ethan waited until Trey was halfway back to the garage before emerging from the shadows. He'd timed it perfectly. Far enough from the house to avoid cameras, close enough to the garage that Trey couldn't easily ignore him.

"Mr. Spalding," he called in low tones. "Got a minute?"

Trey's steps never faltered, but his head turned to the new voice. "The service entrance is around back, and we're not hiring."

"Even for old friends?" Ethan stepped into the light. "Seven years is a long time, Trey. Thought you might want to catch up."

Trey stopped, his posture still perfect. "Riley." He spoke the name like it tasted bitter. "Heard you were out."

"Two weeks ago." Ethan glanced toward the mansion. "Place looks good. Quiet. Like that night."

"We don't discuss that night." Trey's voice could have frozen boiling water. "Ever."

"Fair enough." Ethan raised his hands in surrender. "I'm just looking for work. Good work. The kind Dakota and I used to do."

"Dakota Bloodworth is gone." Something flickered in Trey's eyes. Concern? Warning? "Left town years ago, right after you went inside. Myanmar, last I heard. Or maybe Tibet."

Ethan's laugh was sharp. "Funny. That's where I hear the young Mr. Boucheron is, too."

The garage lights shone across Trey's face, catching the slight tightening around his mouth. He studied Ethan for a long moment, then gestured toward the side door. "Come in. Briefly."

The garage apartment looked exactly as Ethan remembered: tasteful, minimal, everything in its place. Trey moved to a cabinet that Ethan knew held excellent, eighteen-year-old Scotch.

"You're not welcome here," Trey said, pouring two fingers into a crystal tumbler. "But I owe you this much: Leave Silvergrove. Tonight. There's nothing for you here anymore."

"Nothing?" Ethan accepted the scotch. "Not even answers about what happened to Ursula? Or where that pretty red cat ended up?"

"Mrs. Boucheron died of natural causes." Trey's voice was flat. "The coroner was quite clear. Cancer."

"Sure. Just like Dakota went to Tibet." Ethan sipped his scotch. "Come on, Trey. We both know there's more to it. That job was supposed to be simple. In and out, grab and go. Instead, Ursula dies, Dakota vanishes, and I take the fall. Seven years, Trey. I had a lot of time to think about that night."

"And I've had seven years to build something here." Trey's perfect posture cracked. "Whatever you think you know, whatever you're planning, don't. Some questions are better left unanswered."

A soft chime sounded from the intercom connected to the main house. "Trey?" Val's words slurred. "Bring the car around. I need to go to Casa Sol."

"Of course, Miss Boucheron. Right away." Trey set down his untouched Scotch. "We're done here, Riley. Take my advice about

27

leaving. Now. Tonight." He moved to the door, then paused. "And don't bother the flower shop. Whatever you're thinking, it won't end well."

Ethan finished his Scotch, savoring the burn. How did he know he'd watched old lady Brannigan's lair? Through the garage windows he saw Trey guide the Rolls Royce up the curved drive to the main entrance. Val emerged, draped in something expensive and flowing, already unsteady on her feet despite the early hour.

Seven years, he thought. Seven years in prison while everyone else walked away. They owed him, and he would collect. He set the empty glass on Trey's immaculate counter and slipped out into the darkness. He had no intention of leaving Silvergrove. Not until he knew the truth about that night, about Dakota, about the red jade cat that had cost him seven years of his life.

Besides, he thought, something was definitely happening at Brannigan's Bloomers. And if Trey was worried about him watching the place, well, that just meant he was onto something.

The Monday night lights at Edson Keating High blazed against the spring darkness, casting sharp shadows across the harsh aluminum bleachers. Soccer wasn't football in Texas, but it still drew a decent crowd, especially with the Koalas heading toward district finals. Ethan Riley lingered at the edge of the parking lot, watching the steady trickle of late arrivals hurrying toward the field.

He spotted his marks easily enough: the cluster of teenagers in the top corner of the home stands. The girl with the expensive haircut had to be Ryan Ruggle; he'd seen her at Casa Sol earlier. Next to her sat a tall, lanky boy cradling a guitar, another kid with thick glasses bent over what looked like math homework, and the curly-haired girl who'd been running the morning before. Verona, if he remembered right from his surveillance near City Lake. And some chick who looked foreign, that had to be Cheryl.

The boy sitting apart from the others caught Ethan's eye. The pressed chinos, the too-neat fade haircut, the calculated distance from the group. Street fashion from a decade ago, when Ethan had last seen it. Ethan watched a moment more as the youngster twiddled a closed switchblade.

Ethan climbed the bleachers, careful to project just the right mix of confidence and casualness. He dropped onto the bench one row below the tough kid, angling his body toward the field.

"Hell of a game," he offered, nodding toward the action.

The boy, who couldn't be more than sixteen, glared at Ethan. Ethan waited. He knew intimidation from his prison years. This wasn't it.

"I ain't here for no stupid game."

"No?" Ethan kept his voice mild. "So what brings you out on a Monday night?" Ethan tilted his head, waiting.

"Gloriano," the kid supplied, then looked like he regretted it. "*El Guapo* to you, Bobo. And I'm waiting for my people."

"Your people?" Ethan allowed a hint of interest to color his tone. "Must be important, missing the game for them."

Gloriano straightened, warming to the attention. "Yeah, we got business. Real business, not this school shit."

The guitar player shifted and struck a low chord. The nerd with the calculus book hunched lower over his homework.

"Business is good," Ethan nodded. "Done some myself. Cars, mostly. Back in the day."

Gloriano leaned in. "For real? Like, chopped?"

"Among other things." Ethan let the implications hang there. "Did some time for it, matter of fact," he lied.

"That's hard, man." Gloriano leaned in, fully engaged now. "We got something going with cars too. And other stuff. Had a fight with some *pendejos* from East Grove last week. Showed them what's what."

Ryan and Verona exchanged glances. The brain, Darwin, Ethan caught someone whisper, closed his book with shaking hands.

Movement at the bottom of the stands caught Ethan's attention. Six figures waited in the shadows, all older than high school age. One wore a red bandana that almost glowed under the stadium lights.

"There's my people," Gloriano stood in a rush. "Gotta bounce."

"Mind if I come along?" Ethan kept his voice casual. "Been looking to make some connections, you know?"

Gloriano hesitated, flattered but uncertain. "Gotta ask Paco. He runs things."

They descended the bleachers together, Ethan feeling the teenagers' eyes on his back. The man in the bandana watched their approach with hooded eyes.

"Who's this?" Paco's voice was soft, dangerous. He held a worn folding knife without overt menace.

"Just got out," Ethan said before Gloriano could speak. "Looking to get back in the game. Heard you might be running some interesting business."

"Out from where?" Paco whispered.

Ethan paused. "Gatesville, then Cotulla. They moved me because I caused a problem." Ethan rolled up his sleeves to show the prison tats he'd earned.

Paco studied him, eyes narrowed. "I heard of you," he said. After a long moment he gave a slight nod. "Come on then. We'll see."

As they melted into the darkness beyond the stadium lights, Ethan heard the explosion of whispers from the bleachers behind them.

"Oh my God," Garrett's voice carried. "Did you see —"

"Who was that guy?" Darwin demanded.

"We have to tell Rick," Verona insisted. "As soon as the game's over."

Cheryl whispered low so almost nobody could hear, "Where's a good shotgun when you need one."

The final whistle pierced the night, sharp and clear. Ethan smiled to himself as he heard the teenagers scrambling down the bleachers, their voices high with excitement and anxiety. Let them talk. By the time Rick heard their story, Ethan would be well on his way to infiltrating Silvergrove's purgatory.

Ahead of him, Paco and his crew moved with practiced stealth, leading him toward whatever "business" awaited. Seven years was long enough to change a man, but not enough to change the work. Cars still got chopped, gangs still fought over territory, and there were always angry young men looking for leadership.

Sometimes, Ethan knew, those angry young men knew things. Things about jade cats, and missing cousins, and wealthy families.

✧ ⊠ ✧ ⊠ ✧

The warm light of Casa Sol felt cozy until Val Boucheron walked in, shattering the spell. Kyle watched her from his corner table. She'd squeezed herself into a burgundy designer dress that was trying way too hard for Silvergrove. Diamond earrings and a matching necklace threw sparkles across the room like a cheap dance hall. Her four-inch heels clicked and wobbled against the stone floor; the kind of shoes that looked like a broken ankle waiting to happen. He watched her, along with most of the staff, and couldn't shake the image of a faded beauty chasing her glory days.

He stood as she approached.

"Ms. Boucheron," he offered, helping her to her seat. He made sure his smile was genuine but careful, the way a man might approach a beautiful but unpredictable animal.

"Val, please." She waved away the formality, her hand moving so erratically it nearly took out a water glass. "And you must call me Val."

The wine steward approached their table, but Val was already gesturing for cocktails before the poor guy could even recite the evening's specials.

"Just club soda for me," Kyle said, then added, "For now."

Val's martini arrived with the appetizers, a duck confit that he approached with polite uncertainty. By the time their entrées appeared, she had switched to some impossibly expensive red wine she'd insisted on ordering for them both. Kyle's glass remained untouched.

"So then I said to Marshall – that's my father, you know – I said he simply had to update the east wing. All those dreary old paintings." Val's words began to slide into each other. "But he's so stuck in the past. Everything's about Ursula's taste, Ursula's collections..."

Kyle pushed his swordfish around his plate, nodding at what he hoped were the right moments. When the dessert menu appeared, he declined with a smile he hoped didn't look as tired as he felt.

31

"Oh, you must try the chocolate soufflé," Val insisted, ordering two for herself. "Unless you'd prefer something sweeter?" Her attempt at a suggestive smile was so forced it was painful.

"Ms. Boucheron — Val," Kyle set down his napkin. "I should probably —"

"Nonsense!" She reached for his hand across the table, bumping her wine glass. "The evening's just starting. I thought we might go back to the mansion. I could show you Ursula's old studio. Nobody ever goes there anymore..."

She shifted in her chair, attempting what he guessed she thought was an alluring pose. Instead, she listed dangerously to one side, her elbow missing the table by inches.

Kyle stood. "I think you've had enough. Of everything."

"Excuse me?" Her voice went cold enough to frost the valley in mid-summer.

"Look, I appreciate the dinner. But I'm not interested in... whatever this is." He gestured at her swaying form. "You're drunk, and I'm not that kind of guy."

"That kind of —" Val pushed herself up, gripping the table for support. "Do you know who I am?"

"Yeah, I do," Kyle said, his face hardening. "And it's not as impressive as you think it is."

He turned to leave, only to find Val's chauffeur, Trey, blocking his path. The man's expression was pleasant, casual, and borderline terrifying.

"Get out of my way," Kyle growled. "Unless you want to step outside and see how things work in the real world."

Trey's smile never wavered as he stepped aside, moving to support Val's increasingly unstable form. "Good evening, Mr. Ferguson. Do drive safely."

Kyle watched as Trey guided Val through the restaurant, her protests fading to mumbles. Through the front windows, he saw Trey deposit her into the Rolls Royce's back seat like a parent handling a sleepy child.

As he rounded his truck, a voice carried across the parking lot. "I know exactly how dangerous the real world is, Mr. Ferguson. Better than most."

Something in Trey's tone made Kyle's spine tingle, but he shook it off as he climbed into his Ford. Probably just another rich lady's lapdog, trying to sound tough.

The Rolls glided away, silent as a specter in the Texas night. Kyle gunned his engine, drowning out the small voice in his head that suggested Trey Spalding might be all bluster, or he might be something far more dangerous than a simple chauffeur.

Chapter Four

Tuesday dawned wet and gloomy, forcing Aileen to dig out the floral-print blouse and black slacks she saved for special occasions. Her work clothes sat in a dejected pile in her car, victims of potting soil, fertilizer, and that unfortunate incident with the leaking watering can.

Not So Fast Dry Cleaners was already open, though Mr. Patel looked like he wished it wasn't.

"No starch," Aileen said, hefting her bag onto the counter. "And I really need these —"

"Thursday." Mr. Patel didn't look up from his ledger.

Aileen poked the bag with a fist. "But all my work clothes are in here. Surely you could —"

"Thursday." He looked up and met her eyes. "Very busy. Easter coming."

"Everyone's got Easter coming," Aileen muttered, but took her claim ticket and dashed to her car.

The rain picked up as Aileen pulled into Bloomers' parking lot. By the time she unlocked the front door, her carefully brushed hair was plastered to her neck, and her good blouse clung uncomfortably to her shoulders.

The ancient coffee maker gurgled ominously when Aileen switched it on. "Come on, old friend," she coaxed, patting its scratched plastic side. "Just one more day. I promise I'll replace you soon." The machine responded with a sound like a dying racoon, but eventually produced something that smelled almost like coffee.

Aileen settled at her desk with the morning's first cup, allowing herself the luxury of the newspaper's crossword. 'Floral arrangement for the deceased (6 letters)' — WREATH. Well, that was practically cheating. Aileen was halfway through the cryptogram when she remembered she needed to flip the sign.

She'd barely gotten the sign flipped over and the lights up when Manville Beadle burst through the door, trailing rain and self-importance. The town's chief intelligence officer, self-appointed, was already talking before he crossed the threshold. Manville's appearance would frighten a blind man, Aileen thought, with permanently unkempt hair, days-old fuzz and old-man dress.

"Did you hear?" He didn't wait for an answer. "Miss Betty saw him plain as day, standing under her oak tree! Called Chief Couch right away, but you know how he is these days. Jumpy as a cat in a room full of bulldogs. Wouldn't even come look!"

"Good morning, Manville," Aileen said with patience she didn't feel, setting down her coffee cup. "Who did Miss Betty see?"

"The felon!" Manville's voice dropped to what he thought was a whisper. Others might charitably think 'bullhorn.' "Ethan Riley! Just got out of prison. Seven years for burglary, they say. Though Miss Betty's cousin's hairdresser swears it was armed robbery. Or maybe murder!" His eyes gleamed with the joy of spreading fresh gossip.

Aileen thought of the shadowy figure she'd seen yesterday evening but kept her face neutral. "I'm sure Chief Couch has it under control."

"Ha!" Manville did a slow pivot, examining every corner of the shop. "You ready for Easter? Lots of valuable merchandise here. Lots of dark corners." He patted his hip where, Aileen knew, he still carried the mall security badge he'd earned twenty years ago. "I could keep an eye on the place at night. Still got my Billy club. And my helmet!"

"That's very kind —"

"No trouble at all!" He puffed out his chest. "I can see everything from my second story. Well, most everything. The loading area's a bit hidden by Miss Betty's oak, but —"

"Manville." Aileen gestured to the stack of orders on her desk. "I'm sorry, but I need to get to work."

"Oh! Oh, of course, of course." He backed toward the door, still scanning the shop. "But you'll let me know if you see anything suspicious? Any strange characters hanging around?"

"You'll be my first call," Aileen assured him, turning to her paperwork.

The doorbell announced his departure and Aileen watched through the rain-streaked sheet glass as Manville hurried across the damp street, probably heading to the diner to share his theories about Ethan Riley with the breakfast crowd. She hoped the nosy old gossip wouldn't catch cold.

Aileen picked up her cup, found it empty, and sighed. The coffee maker chose that moment to make another dying sound. "I know," she told it. "We all have our crosses to bear." Outside, the rain tapped on the shop's roof and windows, while somewhere in Silvergrove a felon wandered free. But orders needed filling, Easter was coming, and life went on.

Aileen had just listed the last number on her EastTex order when the coffee maker sputtered dry. She stared at the empty pot in betrayal. "Tomorrow," she promised herself. "Something with actual capacity."

The door interrupted her coffee maker fantasies. Through the rain-streaked windows she could make out a familiar hunched figure, and her chest tightened.

Scruffy Scruggs stood just inside the entrance, water dripping from his army surplus jacket onto the welcome mat. His eyes darted around the shop before settling somewhere near Aileen's left shoulder. In his massive, scarred hands, two tiny kittens mewed plaintively.

"Morning, Scruffy," Aileen kept her voice soft, gentle. Like talking to a spooked horse. "Those are beautiful kittens you've got there."

"Found 'em." His voice was rusty, as if he didn't use it much. "Behind the Piggly Wiggly. Thought maybe..." He shifted his weight, combat boots squeaking against the wet floor. "Thought maybe you could use 'em. For mice. Shop like this gets mice."

His Piggly Wiggly mention nagged at her. That old grocery closed long before she'd arrived in Silvergrove. Where had he really found the kittens? Her first instinct was to decline, as she had enough on her plate without two tiny lives to care for, to worry about. Something in Scruffy's expression stopped her. He always looked lost, but today there was an extra layer of nervousness in his eyes. Aileen knew better than to ever suggest the pet shelter.

"We could put them in a box under my desk," she heard herself say. "Keep them warm and dry."

Relief flooded his weathered face. Together they gathered an empty orchid crate and some clean rags, Aileen watching Scruffy arrange everything just so. The kittens settled in moments, purring like tiny diesels.

"How's the trapping going?" Aileen asked, watching him stroke one kitten's orange fur with a gentleness that belied his massive hands.

"Ain't much good this time of year." He shrugged his massive shoulders. "Why I'm back in town. Coyotes are moving different now. Everything's... different."

"Have you been over to the VA recently? In Nacogdoches?"

The change was immediate. Scruffy's face darkened, his hands clenching into fists. "They hate me. Think I'm crazy. Think I don't know what I saw over there, what I..." He cut himself off, breathing hard, almost vibrating.

"Here," Aileen said, breaking his outburst while pouring the last of the coffee into a clean mug. "Still hot."

He took the cup with trembling hands, sinking to sit cross-legged on the floor beside the kitten box. His eyes kept darting to the paper bag on Aileen's desk that held her lunch, and to the day-old pastries on the counter.

Without a word, she handed him both. He tried to refuse, but Aileen insisted as she read the hunger in his eyes. "I was going to throw the rolls out anyway," Aileen lied. "And I'm having dinner with... a friend tonight." She didn't mention it was just Andy and a community theater performance, still two days away. And not really a date, she warned herself.

Scruffy tucked everything into his coat pockets, the fabric bulging in odd places. He rose as if late to church, head cocked, listening to sounds only he could hear. "Thank you, ma'am. For the kittens. And..." He gestured at his loaded pockets.

"Any time, Scruffy. You're welcome any time. Take care."

He moved toward the door before she finished, that haunted look back in his eyes. The rain had paused, though darker clouds were building to the west. Aileen watched him shuffle away, his shoulders hunched against enemies no one else could see.

The kittens mewed from their box, and Aileen felt tears pushing at her eyelids. Some wounds, she thought, never healed. Some people carried their storms inside them, no matter what the weather.

✧　ㅂ　✧　ㅂ　✧

Garrett Herbers eased into the stairwell at Keating High, guitar case bumping against his leg. The morning's rain was over, though the stairs were still damp. Lunch hour was his practice time, when he knew the others wouldn't come out to their spot. That new Garth Brooks tune had one chord progression that kept tripping him up. He settled onto the concrete steps, hoping to avoid any staff walking by.

The guitar's strings moved in familiar patterns under his fingers as he worked through the sequence, keeping his strumming quiet. After a few attempts, he set the guitar aside and pulled out yesterday's letter, the envelope worn from multiple readings.

Ray John was on break while the logging crew relocated in the Cascades. His older brother's handwriting sprawled across the page, talking about missing Mom's cooking and asking if Garrett was "finally getting somewhere with that guitar." He could hear Ray John's deep laugh in his mind, the kind of fun that used to fill their kitchen on those rare nights when all three brothers managed to be home at once.

"Any word from James?" Ray John's question jumped off the page. The Bering Sea crab season should have ended by now, but their middle brother's boat hadn't reported in yet. Garrett pushed away the worry that had gnawed at him for days.

The letter ended with Ray John's usual teasing: "Write soon and tell me about that girlfriend you should have by now." Garrett snorted. Like he had time for dating between school, practice, and his weekend gigs at The Rusty Nail.

The warning bell jarred him from his thoughts. He carefully tucked his guitar back in its case, already planning how to stay awake through Patterson's algebra class. Maybe he could work out that bridge section in his head while pretending to care about quadratic equations.

The afternoon dragged, each hour marked by soft mewing from under Aileen's desk. She'd fed the kittens some warm milk, but her own stomach protested its empty state. That lunch she'd given Scruffy was a distant memory.

Rain drummed an even beat on the greenhouse roof as Aileen checked the Easter lily shipment for signs of blight. The door tones pulled her to the front sales area, water dripping from her sleeve as she rounded the corner.

A young man stood just inside, rainfall beading on his new Astros hoodie. Something about his stance made her miss a step. The way he occupied the space like he owned it, perhaps, or the smile that lived only on his lips, never going near his eyes. His dark brown hair looked artfully disheveled, the kind of casual that took time to achieve. Designer jeans and premium running shoes completed the curated image of casual wealth.

Before she could offer a greeting, he spoke. "So this is the great Aileen Freakin' Brannigan." His eyes swept the shop like a prosecutor gathering evidence. "Pretty place. Must take a lot of work."

The words landed like slaps. Aileen felt her spine stiffen, rooted to the spot by his tone.

"I'm Dakota." He watched her face for any response. "Where's Ethan?"

The name hit her like cold water. She could only shake her head, mouth gone dry.

"He said he'd meet me at our special place. His last place, before they put him away. A hiding place." A sly smile crawled across Dakota's face. "That's around here, somewhere."

"I... I don't know any Ethan," Aileen managed. "What can I do for you?"

"Give him a message." Dakota's voice hardened. "Tell him I'll be back Wednesday." He took a step closer. "And you better get it right."

He turned to leave, his shoulder catching a large ceramic pot. The dracaena crashed to the floor, terracotta shattering across the tiles. Soil scattered like dark blood.

"Oops." Dakota's smile was pure malice now. With deliberate slowness, he reached out and pushed over a display of hand trowels and pruning shears. They clattered across the floor like falling silverware.

"Don't forget," he called over his shoulder as he stepped into the rain.

Aileen watched through the front windows as he strolled away, unaffected by the downpour, as if attacking small businesses was just another item on his daily agenda. The kittens mewed from their box, and somewhere in the back of her mind, she wondered how anything about Bloomers could be special to a couple of thugs.

Aileen looked down at the broken pot, the scattered tools, the mess that would take an hour to clean. But it wasn't the destruction that made her hands shake. It was the realization that, without wanting to, without even knowing how, she'd been pulled into whatever dark game Ethan Riley was playing.

And Dakota, whoever he was, clearly knew the rules better than she did.

The phone call with Mavourneen left Aileen feeling hollowed out, an empty shell. "Yeah, Mom, everything's fine," Mav said, distracted by something in her Durham apartment. "Look, I've got to go. Meeting friends for dinner." The distance between them grew with every conversation, stretching far beyond the thousand miles that separated them. Sometimes Aileen wondered if the divorce had broken more than a marriage, leaving an unfixable space between them.

A piercing crash from the front of the shop destroyed her melancholy. Glass shattered, followed by the wet smack of plants hitting tile. Aileen rushed from her office into bedlam.

Black-masked figures moved through her shop like wraiths given form, destroying everything in their path. Orchids scattered like broken butterflies. A display of hanging baskets crashed to the ground, painting color across the floor. Shelves shrieked as they tore loose from the walls.

"There!" One of the masked men pointed, and two figures peeled away from the destruction, heading straight for her.

Aileen scrambled back into her office, slamming the door. Her hands shook as she fumbled for her phone. The door shuddered once, twice, then burst inward with a crack of splintering wood. Her phone slipped from her hand, the screen showing a half-dialed number.

Aileen curled into the corner, making herself as small as possible. Rough hands seized her hair, yanking her up until her feet barely touched the ground. Through tears of pain, she saw the metallic flash of a switchblade.

"Where is it?" The voice behind the mask was young and angry. When Aileen only whimpered, he shook her harder. "WHERE?"

The blade swept across her upper left arm, leaving a streak of fire. Pain bloomed, and Aileen felt the sticky warmth of her own blood leaking onto her forearm. Her elegant floral blouse. Ruined.

"I don't..." Aileen gasped. "I don't know what you want."

The assailant threw her into the corner. Aileen folded into the corner, clutching her bleeding arm. "The treasure," he snarled. "The goods Ethan promised. Hand it over, or I'll open your throat."

Something sparked in Aileen then, a flash of defiance born of terror and confusion. They'd violated her place, her life. "You won't get anything if I'm dead."

"She's right," the second masked man said, his voice uncertain. "We need her alive to —"

Sirens wailed in the distance, growing closer.

"Out the back!" the first attacker ordered. "Smash everything!"

They vanished like smoke, leaving devastation behind them. More crashes came from the back of the shop and the greenhouse, along with the sound of running feet. In seconds, silence replaced the chaos, broken only by Aileen's voiceless sobs and the steady drip of water from overturned plants.

The kittens whimpered in their box, untouched in the chaos. Aileen pressed her right hand against her bleeding arm and wailed. Not from pain, but against violation. Her shop, her sanctuary, destroyed by shadows hunting treasure she knew nothing about.

The sirens drew closer. Aileen barely heard them. All she could think about was Ethan Riley, and whatever door to Hades he'd kicked open in her life.

✧　✠　✧　✠　✧

Rick's skateboard clattered across broken glass as he burst through the doorway, nearly colliding with Chief Couch. His howl of anguish echoed off the ravaged walls. "AILEEN!"

"Easy, son," Couch said, pressing a compress against Aileen's arm while speaking into his radio. "She's right here. She'll be fine."

"Let me," Rick choked out, hands reaching for the compress. Couch nodded and stepped away, giving instructions about crime scene photography to Delilah Ellis, his jailer and temporary deputy.

"My God, Aileen." Rick's voice cracked as he held the compress. "Who did this? I'll kill them. I swear I'll —" He dissolved into tears. "You've been more mom to me than... than..."

Aileen found herself laughing through her own tears. "Language, Richard," she managed, as creative curses tumbled from his mouth. Aileen had never heard him swear before. He appeared to have a talent for it.

Dr. Valentine Laetner arrived in yoga pants and a University of Texas sweatshirt, her medical bag clutched in one hand. Dr. Laetner moved Rick aside, her gentle, long fingers examining the wound. Rick retreated to a corner, alternating between sniffles and muttered profanity that would make a ship's captain take notes.

The teens arrived as a unit: Jessie, Verona, Cheryl, Darwin, and Garrett, all hovering just inside the doorway like uncertain birds. Rick went to update them, and something in their gathered presence seemed to break a dam in Silvergrove.

People began trickling in, first to stare at the destruction, then to act. Ephron Dewitt appeared with a push broom and began organizing volunteers. "Let Delilah work, folks! Kyle, start gathering those intact pots. Terilynn, can you sweep that section? Careful of the glass..."

The door rattled frequently as more townspeople arrived. Fagan, his wife Ciara, and Charity brought boxes for salvageable inventory. Andy stood in the doorway looking stricken until someone handed him a mop. Marlene Niedermayer bustled in with cardboard carriers of coffee from the diner, passing them out like communion.

Aileen watched from her perch on a wooden stool, her arm bandaged and aching. The shop that had been a war zone an hour ago transformed under the hands of her neighbors. Someone rescued orchids, setting them upright in the greenhouse. Kyle and two other men measured the broken windows for temporary boards.

"You need to see the emergency clinic," Dr. Laetner said, concern coloring her professional voice. "Then home and rest. And I want you in my office early tomorrow."

Aileen shook her head. "The clinic's open all night. I can't leave yet..."

Two hours later, darkness had fallen and the impromptu cleanup crew had done all they could. They gathered in the parking lot, talking in low voices about the attack, sharing theories and fears. Chief Couch approached Aileen with an evidence box.

"I'll take the register and records to the station," he said. "Keep them safe."

"Thanks, Roland," Aileen said. "I forgot to mention, a man named Dakota stopped by before all this."

Couch grimaced, then relaxed. "Okay, use Roland. We've known each other long enough. Isn't Dakota the name of Ethan's cousin?"

Aileen shrugged, exhaustion and delayed shock making her sway on her feet. Andy appeared at her elbow. "Come on," he whispered. "Let's get you to the clinic."

As Andy guided her to his car, Aileen looked back at her shop. Plywood covered the broken windows, and trash bags bulged with broken pottery and ruined plants. Something else filled the space now. The echo of helping hands, of a community that had rushed to her aid without being asked.

The parking lot emptied, though the conversations would continue across dinner tables and front porches throughout Silvergrove. Someone had attacked one of their own, had violated their peace. Someone would pay.

For all its small-town quirks, gossip and petty drama, Silvergrove took care of its own.

Chapter Five

Margaret Holloway's arthritis made morning visits to her husband's grave a slow, deliberate process. At seventy-eight, she moved with the careful precision of someone who knew each step might be her last. Reverend Robert Holloway had been buried just three days earlier. In spite of her loss, Margaret maintained their decades-long routine of fresh flowers and morning prayers, ensuring everything remained perfect.

Silver Hill Cemetery sprawled across three gentle hills, oak trees casting long shadows in the early morning light. The cemetery had been part of Silvergrove longer than most families could remember, each grave a testament to the town's history.

The cool spring air made a wispy mist that lay about two feet thick along the ground. A few birds sang in the trees, fewer than Margaret expected in spring. She strolled, in no hurry, her cane tapping in cadence with her foot. She didn't mind the longer walk; they had chosen the two plots, side by side, years ago, as it placed them in the shadier part of the memorial park. It gave her time to reminisce about their lives together, the good and the bad, the fifty-nine years of marriage, two lovely children and now a whole flock of youngsters across generations. She smiled and thanked the Lord for their time in service together.

Margaret felt something was wrong before she saw the body. The morning air carried a metallic tang, something underneath the usual scents of damp earth and new spring growth. Her walking stick began to tap an uneven rhythm against the stone path as she faltered in confusion, each step bringing her closer to Robert's grave.

First she saw a shoe. Then an ankle. Then the entire body, draped across her husband's freshly covered plot.

The young man lay face-down, positioned with a precision that suggested intention rather than accident. His left hand hung over the grave's edge, fingers almost touching the new-mown grass. His dark jacket was muddy, one sleeve torn at the shoulder.

Margaret's arthritic fingers tightened on her walking stick. She'd seen death before; she was a reverend's wife, after all. But this felt different. Wrong.

Her scream was soft at first, then built to a pitch that startled nearby sparrows into flight. The cemetery groundskeeper, Old Tom Reilly, came running, his morning coffee sloshing from a thermos.

"Sweet ten-pound baby Jesus," Tom muttered, crossing himself despite being only nominally religious. He'd seen plenty in forty years of tending graves, but never a scene like this.

Within thirty minutes, Silver Grove's essential law enforcement presence, which meant Chief Couch and Acting Deputy Delilah, had cordoned off the area. Crime scene tape fluttered like morbid bunting, yellow against the green of early spring.

Margaret said she felt faint, and Tom ran to the shack to get a folding chair. She sat in a slump, watching the two peace officers study and mutter, step and bend as they investigated. Delilah had her camera going, the flash spreading like lightning in the slowly-disappearing, wispy ground fog. When the coroner's hearse arrived, the two men who came with it waited outside the crime scene tape until Chief Couch dismissively gestured for them to take the body.

By mid-morning, the hearse, the fog, and all the evidence were gone, but rumors had spread faster than spring dandelions. At the Classy Cook Café, at the Post Office, in business parking lots and school hallways, one question dominated: Who was the dead man, and why was he left on Reverend Holloway's grave?

Margaret returned home, her walking stick tapping a dirge. She'd arrange fresh flowers for Robert later. Right now, she needed a cup of strong tea and time to calm her fluttering heart.

The body was identified by mid-afternoon: Ethan Riley, newly released from prison. But in Silvergrove, identification was just the beginning.

Silver Hill Cemetery no longer welcomed visitors in the harsh morning light. Silvergrove's temporary deputy moved like a pale ghost between the tombstones, her white protective suit a stark contrast to the green grass and weathered granite markers.

"Look at this," Delilah Ellis called, crouching near the edge of Reverend Holloway's grave. Her gloved hand pointed to a series of minute fibers caught in the disturbed earth. Dark blue. Expensive fabric. "Doesn't match the victim's clothing." She placed her camera on the neighboring headstone, took out an evidence pouch and tweezers, and captured the fibers.

Chief Couch grunted, more interested in the body bag being loaded into the county van. His right hand rested in his hip pocket, a response Delilah had noticed before when Couch confronted death. The reminder of that second bullet that had nearly taken his life was still strong after all these years.

"Trace of expensive cologne," she continued, snapping close-up photographs. "Very distinctive. Not Riley's style." She pulled out another evidence bag, collecting microscopic fragments of soil that didn't match the grave's.

Couch put his hands on his hips and huffed, scanning all around. "How would you know Ethan's style?" he asked.

Delilah smiled at her boss. "Okay, maybe I'm assuming too much. A felon, wearing clothes from K-Mart or somewhere, in beat-up tennies, and he's sporting an expensive cologne? Doesn't make sense." She returned to capturing a complete photo collage of the area.

The body had been positioned with care: face down, stretched across the fresh, grassless dirt. No obvious wounds. No immediate cause of death visible. Just the torn jacket and a little mud. With the rains yesterday, that was expected.

"Looks like he was killed somewhere else," Delilah muttered, more to herself than to Couch. "Then transported and positioned."

"You know that how?" Couch challenged. Delilah didn't lose her patience with the Chief. She never lost her patience with him, she understood his foibles and their source.

"Okay, if you're right, then there will be tire tracks after yesterday's rain." Couch began a close inspection of the road's edge.

"That's interesting." She pointed. A partial shoe print near the grave's edge caught her attention. Not a work boot, not a running shoe. Something more refined. Expensive. She photographed it from several angles, knowing half the evidence would be lost by the time it reached the lab.

Couch wasn't listening. "Aileen Brannigan," he muttered. "She's got motive. Recent attack. Connection to Riley."

"Chief," Delilah said, "we've got trace evidence suggesting this was a professional job. Look at the positioning. Look at these fibers. Besides," she wondered, "how would she do it? Beat him to death with gardenias?"

Couch had already made up his mind. The shoe print, the expensive fibers, the distinctive cologne. All of it became background noise to the story he wanted to tell.

"Get me Brannigan's file when we get back," he told Delilah. "I want to bring her in."

Delilah watched him walk away, evidence bags dangling from his fingertips. She knew there wasn't any 'Brannigan's file' at the office. Something about this didn't add up. Not even close.

✧ ¤ ✧ ¤ ✧

Chief Couch's office looked like a tornado had swept through a records retention warehouse. Photographs of Ethan Riley's body were pinned haphazardly across a corkboard, connected by red strings that made sense only to Couch. His left hand, the one that usually rubbed where his missing earlobe should be, traced the connections, fingers wiggling with nervous energy.

"He's got priors," Couch muttered to Delilah, who watched him with a mixture of patience and professional concern. "Burglary. Just out of prison." He peered at the piece of tattoo that stuck out from under Riley's shirt, a clear photograph that Delilah was proud of. She was always proud of her evidence photos.

Delilah knew better than to interrupt when Couch was in one of his spirals. His PTSD from the Big Rig truck stop shooting years ago meant his investigations often looked more like conspiracy theories than solid police work. He sometimes got it right, but even a blind pig could find acorns.

"Aileen Brannigan," Couch announced. "She was attacked just yesterday."

Delilah nodded. "Ethan Riley could be connected to that attack somehow. Didn't she say Dakota was at her shop?"

"Yeah, some minor vandalism," Couch confirmed. "Asked her about Ethan."

Couch started waving his hands. "Aileen, she's our prime suspect. Has to be."

Delilah raised an eyebrow. "Chief, that's a stretch. She was at the clinic when Ethan was killed, if the coroner got the time of death right. Multiple witnesses."

Couch was already reaching for his phone. The name of Silvergrove's most respected business owner meant nothing compared to his need to close a case now.

An hour later, Aileen sat across from Couch in the interview room, her arm neatly bandaged from the previous day's attack. Fluorescent lights made her look ghostly. Her eyes focused on Couch with a focus that made him increasingly uncomfortable.

"Where were you between midnight and 3 AM?" Couch demanded.

"At home," Aileen said. "Alone. No, wait. I didn't leave the clinic until after 2 AM, they were busy with two car accident victims and I had to wait."

"Anyone who can verify that?"

"No." Her voice was calm. Too calm. "Or would you take Andy Burrell's word?"

Couch leaned forward. The case was solving itself. Aileen Brannigan, respected businesswoman, recent attack victim, no alibi. Perfect.

What he didn't see was the careful calculation behind Aileen's eyes. She knew what Roland Couch was doing. And she wasn't going to make it easy for him.

The north stairwell of Keating High had always been neutral territory. No teachers patrolled here, no administrators saw fit to interrupt the sacred space where teenage conspiracies were born. Jessie Burnsides spread her notebook across her knees, her after-school gas station shift forgotten in the urgency of the moment. She'd make her excuses with her boss Harold Lendon later. He'd understand.

Darwin "Brain" Henslee arrived next, his tablet already humming with preliminary research. "I've compiled everything I can find about Ethan Riley," he announced, pushing his thick-framed glasses up his nose. "Cross-referenced with local crime reports, social media mentions, everything." He sat a couple of steps lower than Jessie.

Garrett Herbers strummed a harsh chord on his guitar as he appeared below, more nervous energy than music. The instrument was his security blanket, something to hold onto when the world felt too complicated. Nobody ever minded his music, and nobody could remember seeing Garrett without his axe.

"We're missing Ryan," Verona observed. She'd noticed Ryan's increasing distance over the past couple of days, the way she'd become more secretive, more withdrawn. Ever since that meal at Casa Sol. Ryan's extravagance still bothered Verona.

"She's been weird lately," Garrett muttered. "Ever since last week."

"What did you see?" Cheryl asked.

"Well, I was driving by the private road that goes up to the Boucheron place, right? And there was Ryan, almost out of sight, going to the mansion."

"Maybe she's just curious," Jessie put in. "Everybody's curious about that old place. Some think it's haunted."

Darwin's laptop flickered as he changed programs. A rudimentary suspect matrix appeared, with Gloriano Saltillo positioned dead center. Red lines connected him to multiple data points: the soccer game encounter with Ethan, known gang associations, suspicious movement around town.

"Look," Darwin said, his voice clinical. "Gloriano was the last person seen with Ethan Riley. That we know of. At the soccer game, remember? And now Ethan's dead. I've got him as the most likely, with an 82.7 percent chance it's him, based on what we know now."

Jessie leaned forward. Her part-time job at the gas station had given her street-smart intuition the others lacked. "Something's not right. Gloriano's connected, but he doesn't seem like a killer."

"Everyone's a killer if the circumstances are right," Garrett said, surprising them with his sudden darkness. "Take that woman way up north. Lizzie Borden, that's her."

"Acquitted," Darwin stated.

"Not the same thing as she was innocent," Verona challenged. Darwin gave her a blank look, nodded agreement, and went back to his spreadsheet.

"We should find Mister Glorified Saltillo and get him to confess!" Cheryl pressed. "Anybody know where he hangs this late in the day?"

"Auto shop," Darwin stated without looking up.

Garrett rose and pushed his guitar onto his back. "Well, let's go before he gets away." The teens packed up their gear and started around to the trades shops.

They found Gloriano behind the auto shop building, looking more nervous than tough. His carefully cultivated image – pressed slacks, perfect haircut, white t-shirt with cigarette pack rolled into one sleeve – seemed to have slipped. A smoke dangled from his fingers, more prop than habit.

"We know something's going on," Jessie challenged, stepping forward.

Gloriano's eyes darted between them. "You know nothing."

"Ethan Riley's dead," Darwin blurted. "And you were the last person to see him alive."

Something broke in Gloriano's expression. Not guilt. Not confidence. Pure, raw fear.

"Back off," he said, but his voice trembled. He reached into his right pocket but didn't pull out his knife.

Garrett stepped forward, guitar forgotten. "We're not backing off. What do you know?"

Gloriano bolted. Not walking away. Not trying to explain. Full-speed running, backpack abandoned, cigarette forgotten on the concrete. The teens watched him disappear, exchanging looks of surprise and confusion.

"That wasn't the reaction I expect of someone who's guilty," Verona said. "That was the reaction of a terrified kid."

Darwin's fingers flew across his tablet. "I'm tracking his social media. There isn't a lot, but something's wrong. Really wrong."

Jessie gathered Gloriano's abandoned backpack. "We need to figure this out before Chief Couch makes a mistake. Before someone else gets hurt."

The bell rang, signaling the end of the school day. But for these five teenagers, the real investigation was just beginning.

Later that afternoon, they would bring their jumbled evidence to Aileen Brannigan. And Aileen would challenge everything they thought they knew about Ethan Riley, Gloriano Saltillo, and the dangerous game being played in Silvergrove.

Squealing brakes announced the arrival of Garrett's Corolla into Aileen's driveway. She turned her attention from her notes to peer out her kitchen window. Garrett killed the engine and got out while Darwin exited from the passenger side. Jessie and Verona climbed out of the back seat on one side, Rick and Cheryl on the other. Aileen smiled at the thought of them all crammed into the Corolla.

Jessie carried a bag from Norton's 7-Eleven, rustling with promise. Garrett exchanged a look with Darwin that suggested this was more than a casual visit. Garrett retrieved his guitar case and a sweating pitcher of lemonade from the trunk. Rick lifted a cardboard box from the back and closed it.

Aileen met the teen brigade at her front door, holding her bandaged left arm slightly away from her body. "Verona's cookie idea," Rick muttered, lifting a flap on the box, revealing a treasure trove of warm chocolate chip sweetness.

"We brought necessities," Verona announced, pushing past Garrett with a determination that brooked no argument. She found a tray in Aileen's kitchen, arranging the cookies with military alignment before pouring lemonade into mismatched glasses that had been in Aileen's family for generations.

"Hydration and sustenance for our investigative conference," Jessie announced. "And some pastries for later," she added, waving the bag she carried.

Darwin adjusted his glasses. "Statistically, sugar improves cognitive processing by 17.3 percent."

Jessie rolled her eyes. "You and your percentages. Do you have the percentages for statistics-induced injuries?" Jessie made a small fist and gave her best mock-angry glare. Everyone chuckled except Darwin.

Darwin pulled prescription-strength pain medication from his backpack. "My mom sent these. Says they're better than the clinic's prescriptions."

Aileen started to protest, then saw the genuine care in their faces. These weren't employees, part-time helpers, or casual friends. They were something more. A family of sorts. True family.

Garrett strummed soft chords on his ever-present guitar, creating a musical backdrop to their serious discussion. The late afternoon light filtered through lace curtains, casting soft shadows across Aileen's living room, a space that spoke of years of careful maintenance and quiet memories. The teens overlooked the bits of detritus here and there. They understood Aileen's time demands, trying to make Bloomers work, and besides, she was injured now.

"Suspects," Darwin said, opening his laptop, already pulling up spreadsheets. A digital suspect matrix appeared, complete with photographs and interconnecting lines. Aileen was impressed with how much neater Darwin's board was than Couch's. "We need to systematically analyze potential murderers."

Aileen sat in her comfortable recliner, old and battered, inherited from her dad. "Who do you have on your list?"

Darwin looked up. "How do you want them listed? Least to most likely, or reverse? Or alphabetical?"

Aileen smiled in spite of her arm. Darwin was an amazing young genius, a couple of years younger than any of his friends or classmates. He'd skipped those years in middle school, though all the older kids accepted him. Respected him. They liked his no-nonsense, fact-based approach, and he never made anybody feel bad for not knowing something.

"How about random order?" Aileen playfully suggested.

Darwin nodded and pushed a button. "Okay, first up is Valerian Boucheron. Volatile. Alcoholic. Married three times, divorced three. Connected to the original burglary that put Ethan in prison. Potential motive, unclear execution. The other data I have, though mostly rumor, is that Val was an item with Ethan before he went to prison."

All the teen's faces peered at Aileen, waiting for her royal pronouncement. She realized she must be the leader of this session, not because of her age, but because the teens respected her opinions and thoughts. She didn't feel like being an adult today, though. She sighed and continued.

"Val Boucheron. Let's see. She's what, forty-something? Rich. You think she'd have the strength to kill a man?"

Garrett spoke up. "If it was poison? Maybe Ethan wanted to get back together and Val did him in with a drink."

"Darwin, do we have anything from the coroner yet on cause of death?" Aileen asked. Darwin shook his head. Aileen knew the youngster had the ability and no real qualms about hacking into the official databases to get what he needed. She wanted to disapprove, but they needed the data.

"Okay, we leave Val on the list for now, but I don't find it credible. Unless he attacked her, she'd have no motive, and then it wouldn't be poison, would it. Who's next?"

Darwin looked at his screen. "Andrew Burrell."

Aileen jerked upright, eyes bulging. "What?"

Jessie couldn't resist. "Andy Burrell is definitely suspected... of being totally in love with you."

Aileen blushed immediately, heat rising to her cheeks and ears. The teens exchanged knowing looks, their collective smirk speaking volumes about the obvious attraction Aileen hadn't acknowledged was possible.

"Uhh, evidence?" Aileen tried to get the talk back on track, hoping to show the kids how to set emotion aside and think.

"He was devastated when he worked the cleanup yesterday," Verona noted.

Rick took up the prod. "And you're going on dates now, right?" He was almost laughing at his adopted mom, showing how much he'd recovered from yesterday's trauma.

Aileen's blush deepened against her wishes. "Well, once you reach our age, you begin to appreciate the value of friendship," she tried.

The teens looked at each other and realized the gag had gone far enough. "Okay," Verona said, "he's off the list." Aileen sighed, relieved.

Darwin pressed some keys, then said, "Done. Next is Rick."

Rick nearly fell out of his chair. "You little four-eyed runt," he started, then subsided at a small gesture from Aileen. She shook her head and he settled back, still tense.

"Rick, you need to set emotions aside when solving a puzzle like this. If there's evidence, you have to consider it."

Rick sat up straight. "Okay, *Brain*, state your case. And you better have a good one." He flexed his fingers.

"Rick could be a suspect," Darwin said clinically, "if you squint and ignore logic. The only possible black mark is the damage to Bloomers as motive. Okay, and Aileen's injury, but those go together. I can't find anything, social media or whatever, that makes the case." He pushed some keys. "Okay, you're cleared."

Rick just realized he'd been played by Darwin and the group, just as Aileen had. He relaxed and nodded. Aileen could see her young employee mentally marking up a score to be settled later.

"What about that Dakota guy?" Cheryl asked. "Did he come back today?" She remembered overhearing the story Aileen had told Chief Couch.

"Haven't a clue," Aileen said. "Wouldn't matter anyway, nobody at Bloomers." The teens nodded.

"So is he off the list?" Darwin asked, finger poised on the delete key.

Garrett strummed a minor chord that grabbed attention. "Ethan's cousin. Mysterious. Threatening."

"I believe that's enough to leave him on the list," Aileen said. Darwin moved to confirm. "Who's left?"

"Gloriano's our primary suspect," Jessie stated. "He was with Ethan at the soccer game. He ran away when we tried to talk to him. Left his backpack and everything."

Aileen's eyebrow arched. "Running isn't confession, dear. Sometimes it's fear."

"And sometimes it's guilt." Darwin's fingers flew across the keyboard. Gloriano's photo sat center stage, connected to various data points by red lines that looked like a conspiracy theorist's dream. "Plenty of data, ma'am. I vote we leave him on the list."

"Okay, but I challenge you smart kiddos to learn more about Gloriano and see if he's really committed to that gang or not. Associating with Ethan once isn't a conviction. Here's a secret: I almost hired him last summer."

Verona asked, "Really? *Him*?"

Aileen nodded. "His uncle vouched for him, and I know he's a hard worker. Not everybody's cut out to be a great student," Aileen finished, squinting at Jessie.

The teens considered her charge in silence.

Verona asked, "When will Bloomers open again?"

Aileen welcomed the conversation shift. Easter loomed only days away. Bloomers had to get operational soonest.

"Thursday, tomorrow," Aileen said, her voice tight with stress. "Suppliers are coming. Big deliveries."

Rick stepped in. "I'm skipping school. You can't manage alone."

Aileen wanted to protest, but she saw the resolve in Rick's eyes. "Even with your help I don't know how I'll cope. So much damage."

Darwin spoke next. "If you stay closed?"

"If I can't get open tomorrow, then Easter in Silvergrove won't be nearly as pretty this year."

"We'll help," Jessie said. "I can skip school too."

"We all will," Verona added.

Darwin was already drafting a schedule on his laptop. Color-coded, cross-referenced, with backup plans and contingencies. "I've got a rotation mapped. Cheryl and Jessie, you get to contact any of the Tuesday night cleanup crew you can remember."

"But payment —" Aileen started.

"Nope," they chorused.

"And your classes?" she pushed. She refused to wilt under pressure from these intransigent youths.

"All our teachers are good with it," Verona said, fingers crossed behind her back. "They'll look the other way at roll call, as long as you'll vouch that we didn't play hooky."

She gave in with a tired sigh. "Deal," Aileen said, relief in her voice.

A car door slammed outside. Verona's smirk suggested exactly who had arrived.

Andy Burrell walked up the path, a casserole dish in hand, looking simultaneously nervous and hopeful. The teens' collective snicker completed Aileen's embarrassment.

Community, Aileen realized, wasn't just about surviving. It was about showing up. About taking care of each other, one cookie and one casserole at a time.

"Class dismissed," Aileen announced, as she stood to shoo her young friends out. Tomorrow would be a great day.

Chapter Six

Rick turned the key in Bloomers' new lock, pushing the door open and stepping into the abnormally dark front room. He paused with his hand over the light switches, breathing hard. He really didn't want to see how bad the damage was. I have to, he thought. For Aileen. He flipped the lights on.

Rick scanned the room, left to right and back. Not normal, but not bad. With a bit more work he and his friends could run the shop today. There wouldn't be a lot to sell until EastTex delivered, but maybe enough. He walked over to one of the walls, running his hand over a sheet of plywood. The glass panes could be replaced. Their frames hadn't suffered any real damage, he thought. Not being an expert, he held his optimism in check, but hope flickered.

The entrance of his chattering friends washed away his silent musings. Rick enjoyed the energy in the shop as the teens pitched in, reminding him of his grandfather's beehives. He knew they were focused, industrious little rascals, those bees, just like what he saw in Bloomers that morning. He turned to the office to make some reminder calls to suppliers. He had Aileen's list in his pocket.

Ryan Ruggle materialized in the doorway of Bloomers' back office like a ghost, her usual confidence shattered. Rick looked up from the stack of orders in surprise.

"I need to talk," she said, closing the door. Rick waved to the other chair, which she declined, too agitated to sit. She fidgeted and breathed rapidly, completely unlike the self-assured Ryan he knew from school. Her fingers left damp marks on her blouse hem, a nervous gesture that made her look like she was twelve.

"I've done things," Ryan began. "Bad things. And I want out."

"Out of our group?" Rick misunderstood.

"No. I want away from, from the source of the money I've been flashing."

Rick waited, not sure what to do.

"I've just seen what's next for me. Not everything," she clarified. "But enough. Enough that I'm scared." Her eyes darted around the small office. "I can't tell you who my source is. But I want help getting out, away."

"Help how?" Rick asked.

"To stop whatever's happening." She took a deep breath. "With the Boucherons. With the street gang. I don't want to be part of it anymore."

"What can I do?"

"Help me leave Silvergrove, some way that can't be traced by —" she stopped, startled by a crash from the greenhouse.

Before Rick could move, she was gone, leaving only a whisper of fear.

Moments later, an unfamiliar voice came through the same door that Ryan had bolted through. "Good morning," the man said, handing Rick a card. Reward Casualty, Mike Selwyn, Adjuster. His eyes narrowed at Rick and the kittens. "They told me out front that you're in charge. Little young to be running a business?" he asked.

Rick paused, still bothered by Ryan's odd behavior, then he shook Mike's hand, offering a chair. "I'm filling in, the owner's indisposed. How can I help?"

Mike thought for a moment. "Can we get the owner on the phone? Or is he really not available?"

"She," Rick corrected. "Hold on, I know she'll want to speak to you." He dialed her number, then pushed the speakerphone button.

"Hello?" Aileen's clean mezzo-soprano poured from the phone.

"This is Mike Selwyn, ma'am, from Reward Casualty. Your young office manager said he could get ahold of you. Can we chat for a moment?"

"Hi, I'm Aileen Brannigan the owner, and that's Rick, my very special office manager." Rick winced at the title.

"Aileen, I see you've had a rough time the past few days. I'd like to get you a check soon, as I know the meter's running. Isn't this a busy time for gardening?"

"Oh yes, Mike," Aileen confirmed. "A check would help immensely. I've got big orders due in today and tomorrow. What do we do to get that manna from heaven?"

Mike laughed. "Well, I can look around a bit today and get you an interim check early next week. Not the full amount, you understand. But my say-so and some photos will do for starters."

"Thanks," Aileen sighed. Rick heard her prayer winging skyward. "What next, then?"

"We'll need the usual documentation. A comprehensive inventory of losses, cost invoices, incident description. I can tell it's no normal Texas tornado that got you. Oh, and can you get one reliable estimate for the glass replacement?"

"We can do that," Aileen verified. "How soon do you need?"

Mike leaned back a bit. "We're flexible, Aileen. The sooner we get the documentation, the sooner you get paid. Usually takes about ten business days or so, barring complications."

Rick crossed his fingers that 'barring complications' wasn't some sort of delaying tactic. He vowed to have the team pull together the best packet that Mike and Reward Casualty had ever seen, and before the weekend was over. No complications allowed!

Aileen signed off with a quick "Rick's got it" as Mike rose to leave. After another quick handshake Mike toured the rooms to take photos and make notes. Rick liked the guy. He was pleasant and seemed like he wanted to help.

Rick gathered his team and put them to gathering notes and making sketches. Garrett volunteered to secure a glazier's estimate that day. Verona took photos of Garrett's clear sketches and mailed them to Darwin. Rick wanted a detailed story from the group. Darwin said they didn't need a story, he'd already written a four-pager with indices, references, and statistics. The girls chuckled and Darwin's ears went bright red.

Throughout the morning, Silvergrove arrived in waves: helping hands, sympathetic customers, gardeners from miles around. Hands that had cleaned up Tuesday evening now arranged displays, repaired shelving and restocked inventory. The shop hummed with purpose.

Scruffy arrived in utter silence, checking on the kittens. "I brought them milk on Wednesday," he confessed. "Fixed the window I broke," he mumbled. "Didn't want them getting cold."

Rick clenched his jaw at the thought of further damage to Bloomers, and then he read the shame in Scruffy's eyes. "Aileen says thank you," he said, smiling. "For taking care of them."

Just before lunch a car full of young men cruised by, raucous music blasting, windows down. Occupants made threats and gestures. They circled the block three times. The final pass coincided with Chief Couch's cruiser rushing in from the distance, and they vanished.

Rick and Verona watched on the third pass. "Should we be worried?" she asked.

Rick shook his head. After Tuesday, the whole town was watching.

Bloomers was wounded but still standing, and ready to fight.

Rick moved through Brannigan's Bloomers satisfied with what he saw. The day had been a victory. Not just for the shop, but for community resilience. Damaged displays restored. Inventory cataloged. Customers supported. Even a thorough insurance claim prepared.

He unplugged the ancient coffee maker, its faithful service acknowledged with a fond pat, and methodically darkened the rooms. The new temporary door lock, installed Wednesday morning by one of the volunteers, clicked solidly into place. All wasn't well with Bloomers yet, but it was getting there. Rick was pleased with the direction the shop was headed in, and with his role in it.

The parking lot was empty. Dusk settled like cotton wool over Silvergrove, promising another mild spring evening. Rick carried his skateboard out into the gloom as he pondered his changed perception of Verona. She'd been a spark plug all day, keeping the cleanup firing on all cylinders. Flitting here, lifting there, and never complaining. He was ashamed that he'd misjudged her.

Four figures materialized from the shadows between streetlights. The first blow caught Rick across the shoulders, driving him to his knees. The skateboard clattered away into darkness. The attackers circled, clubs rising and falling in a flat, mechanical rhythm. Through the explosion of pain, he heard the whispered message: "Trey sends his regards."

Rick heard the distant siren through a crackling haze, shouting that sounded like it was miles away. The attackers scattered into the dark, leaving Rick in a heap on the asphalt.

Manville Beadle's voice cut through the evening. "Chief! Over here!"

Rick tried to tell Manville what he'd heard, but nothing worked, and then darkness took him.

Aileen stared at her closet. When had dating started to feel less like dressing up and more like defusing a bomb? Her divorce had stripped away more than her marriage; it had dismantled her faith in relationships. Men promised. Men left. Men complicated perfectly good lives.

Andy Burrell is different, a voice whispered. She'd heard those whispers before.

The blue blouse. No, too desperate. The green one. Too casual. She settled on a soft lavender piece with slightly puffy sleeves that her daughter Mavourneen had given her two Christmases ago, before things had gotten complicated. The sleeves meant her bulky bandage wasn't compressed and barely showed. Dark slacks, because she no longer sported a young girl's figure, and comfy but stylish mules finished the ensemble. Well, the mules had been stylish, once, she reflected.

Andy's knock at 6 PM sharp sounded like judgment day. He stood on her porch, shuffling a bit, a single carnation in hand. "For you," he said, looking like a nervous high school student. Aileen marveled at his choice: white, with purple petal tips. How could he have known?

"Pin it?" Aileen asked, turning her shoulder.

Two fumbling attempts later, the flower sat slightly crooked but secure. Like his tie from before.

They filled the drive to Dream Canvas Playhouse with safe small talk, the kind that serves as emotional padding. Andy talked about the school's upcoming science fair, and how the middle school athletes had fared this season. Aileen nodded, watching the Texas twilight, and wondered aloud about tomorrow's weather.

The playhouse felt more like a community center than a theater. Folding chairs. Clean but worn carpet, budget lighting. The energy was pure excitement, though.

"This version," Andy leaned in, whispering, "differs from the movie in some fascinating ways —"

His nervous chatter matched her defensive silence. As a confirmed bachelor, he had no more dating practice than a certain middle-aged divorcée.

The dress rehearsal proceeded as actors found their rhythm. Moments of brilliance punctuated by awkward pauses. The director intervened just once, and very few lines were left behind. A ragged round of applause and kind words for the actors finished the session.

"Dinner?" Andy asked afterward, hope and uncertainty dancing in his voice. They took their time leaving, as there was a tight crowd of well-wishers in the small foyer, each babbling about how their favorite character had come to life. Aileen and Andy both waved at friends and acquaintances. Several folks commiserated with Aileen over the Bloomers situation.

"Sombrero Roja," Aileen decided. Affordable. Familiar. Safe. As long as you stayed away from the five-alarm enchiladas, she reminded herself.

Her phone rang just as they pulled out of the parking lot and headed for highway 21. Chief Couch's number. Aileen prayed it wasn't more trouble at Bloomers.

Couch was sharper than normal, and you could hear excited voices and a siren in his background. "Rick's injured. Gleason Memorial. Now."

Aileen sat as still as if she'd seen Medusa. She couldn't breathe, couldn't move.

"What is it?" Andy asked, concern coloring his usual steady voice.

She found words after several swallows. "It's Rick. My God, they're taking him to Gleason." Silent tears flowed.

Andy nearly put his sedan onto two wheels as he reversed direction. He broke every traffic law between the playhouse and the hospital. Aileen didn't notice, her mind racing with terrible possibilities. She knew guessing was always worse than knowing, but she didn't know, she didn't know.

Once Andy slammed to a stop she burst through the emergency room doors and disappeared. He sat alone in the parking lot with no idea of what to do.

The hospital waiting room muffled sound like a tomb. Aileen's tears came in silent waves as Andy sat nearby, close enough to support but far enough to respect her space. Her phone buzzed relentlessly with messages from worried teens.

Any news?

Is he okay?

Please tell us something!!!

After thirty minutes, Verona burst through the doors, her teenage grief echoing off of sterile walls. "Is Rick okay?" she wailed. Aileen could only hold her and weep while Terry and Rowan watched helplessly from near the entrance before departing with a wave.

Chief Couch appeared moments later, his usual nervous energy amplified. "Any word?" he demanded.

When Aileen shook her head, he stormed into the treatment area like he owned the hospital.

Moments later he returned. "Concussion. Possibly broken arm. They're x-raying his ribs. Potential internal injuries. Overnight stay. Sedated." Couch sat down next to Verona and watched Aileen for reaction.

Andy offered to drive Verona home. She nodded and went quietly, her earlier dramatics replaced by noiseless shock. Couch jumped up and ran when his radio squawked something only he understood.

Alone, Aileen wept silently into a handful of tissues. Her bandaged arm throbbed in sympathy with her broken heart. She couldn't believe the strength of her grief for someone else's son. She had no idea how she'd cope without him.

A nurse approached. "You should go home and rest."

"No!" Aileen's voice cracked. "Sorry, but I'm staying. I'll stay until you let me sit with him. He needs somebody!"

The nurse nodded and led her to Rick's room without a word. Monitors beeped in rhythm with Aileen's racing heart. IV lines dripped. An oxygen mask obscured part of his face.

Aileen barely recognized him beneath the bruising on his face and arms. Only his distinctive hair confirmed it was Rick.

Aileen sat and held Rick's hand. Her tears had dried, replaced by a hard, maternal calm. His family might be absent, but she was here. And she wasn't going anywhere.

Chapter Seven

Three hours of sleep had felt like three minutes. Aileen stared at her untouched scrambled eggs, the coffee growing cold and bitter, much like her thoughts. Rick had awakened around three in the morning, incoherent and in pain. Aileen had watched in silence as the nurse attended to him, then she had excused herself and called a Lyft for home.

Aileen sipped her coffee without tasting. Who would run Bloomers? The shipments were due today. She couldn't afford to lose another day. She couldn't even pay the bill for the flowers, and she'd have to beg for time again. Was the attack on Rick meant for her? Or him? Or something else entirely? Ryan's name kept surfacing, tangled with Rick's mumbled words about Trey. What pit of danger had they all been tossed into?

Her mind spiraled. Each question bred more. The business could collapse. Rick might not recover. The teens, her very own gaggle of misfits, could be in danger.

She paused, a fork of cold scrambleds halfway to her mouth. For just a moment, freedom beckoned. A car. The open road. No responsibilities, no risks. Okay, no job either, she reminded herself. She could call Mav, maybe crash on her couch. Start over somewhere new. Somewhere safe. Maybe that was the way to get Mav back into her heart.

Rick's fragmented hospital mumblings haunted her. "Trey and Ryan... Trey and Ryan..." The nurse's soft sedation had silenced him, but couldn't quiet the questions swirling in Aileen's mind.

Her children, not by blood, but by something just as deep. Darwin with his precise lists. Jessie's fierce loyalty. Garrett's quiet competence. Verona's dramatic heart. Troubled Gloriano. Ryan, dear Ryan: Where could she be? Each teen a puzzle piece in her unexpected clan. Rick at the center, somehow binding them together.

The simultaneous doorbell and knock startled her from her spiraling thoughts.

Garrett stood there, black Stetson in hand, looking both boyish and impossibly mature. Aileen couldn't get her sleep-deprived mind to cough up a reason for his presence. "Uhh, good morning. Did you lose your guitar?"

Garrett chuckled. "I'm opening Bloomers today, with Rick laid up," he said. No drama. No fuss. Just pure, practical support.

When he asked for the new door key, Aileen laughed, half-hysteria, half-relief. Her brigade was mobilizing. She handed over the key that she had recovered from Rick's belongings a few short hours ago. It only felt like days.

Aileen started to offer reminders of where things were and what to do first. Garrett interrupted. "Ma'am," he drawled, "I know where Darwin posted the task list. You can bet he didn't miss anything."

Aileen nodded as Garrett tipped his hat and strode to his beat-up Corolla.

As Garrett's car disappeared down the street, something hardened inside her. This was no longer about survival. This was about justice. She had tried to play it safe, but safe wasn't who she needed to be. Safe wasn't what this community needed. They needed a warrior. For Rick. For the teens. For Bloomers. For herself.

She leaned back in her chair at the dining table. As she relaxed, planning to rest a bit, she remembered her appointment at Northside Bank. She ran to her bedroom, knowing she'd be at least fifteen minutes late now. She hoped her tired face wouldn't scare others away when she arrived.

The bank loan meeting couldn't wait. Neither could her plan to unravel this mystery.

Northside Bank didn't give off its usual cheery, small-town atmosphere today. Aileen knew her history: late payments and small loans, always scraping by. She didn't think she was a bad risk, no more than many other small businesses. No more excuses, she thought as she stood in the lobby. Today she would change trajectory and make Bloomers great.

She walked in like a general, spine straight, eyes focused. No more apologetic shuffling. This was about survival: Bloomers' survival, the teens' survival, her own.

A weird image flashed through her mind, of her wearing Patton's uniform and leading tanks into war. She banished the nonsense. This wasn't World War. It was every bit as threatening to her and the community, though. She nodded and continued forward.

Northside had prints and paintings from local artists, a comfy waiting area, and a big rug in the center that the founder had brought back from Iraq decades ago. Nothing clashed, though the small incongruities whispered small-town. Aileen liked that about Northside. It was decorative enough while still clearly local.

Aileen met her contact only ten minutes late. Felicity Quick looked startlingly like Mavourneen: identical black hair, tall and fit frame, same determined set to her jaw. Only a different eye color: Striking cornflower blue rather than her daughter's Emerald Amaryllis green. Could there really be two? Aileen wondered if the universe was sending her a sign.

Aileen used the social exchange to quiet her heart after the shock of seeing her not-daughter in a bank. Felicity woke up her computer screen and asked why Aileen was visiting Northside today. "$35,000," Aileen said, her voice surprising herself. Steady. Confident.

Her pitch unfolded methodically: advertising, hardware upgrades, full-time staffing, drawing in bold strokes and outlining on the yellow legal pad Felicity provided. Each word was a battle plan, each diagram a strategy. Her old self would have stammered. Today's Aileen spoke with surgical precision.

Felicity typed, watched her screen, and said nothing of consequence.

When Aileen ran out of details, the silence stretched. Aileen's old doubts whispered: Cathay Bank might help. Maybe this was impossible. Run. Escape.

No, she chided the demon, waving a small red creature out of her mind. She was a warrior now. "With your shield or on it" echoed from her ancient history class of way back when. Aileen almost chuckled.

"Your concept is clear, well-considered and thorough," Felicity said. "However, $25,000 is all I can personally authorize," Felicity's face was impassive, hard to read. Her eyes, though; they looked like she'd just lost her puppy.

The old Aileen would have jumped at this sum, and she was inclined to accept gracefully and move on. Today's Aileen asked, "What would it take to get the full amount?" Her heart rate rose. She wished she'd nodded instead.

Felicity made a gesture to hold, then picked up the phone and pushed an intercom button. A few quick words and she hung up. "I'll be back soon, Aileen. Make yourself comfortable. Have some more coffee." She strode out of the office.

Fifteen minutes of nervous waiting, time that good coffee and hope couldn't compress. Felicity returned with a smile and an authorization. She placed the document in front of Aileen. The total of $35,000 appeared at the top. Once seated, Felicity guided Aileen through the signature process, then slipped Aileen's copy into a document cover.

"Patrick wants to keep the only real garden center in Silvergrove open," Felicity said. "He's heard of your plight. It's practically all you hear, out in the lobby."

No collateral required. A gift from the community.

Aileen asked if Felicity could make the deposit or if she should go out to a teller's station. "Oh, I've already transferred the funds," Felicity said. "You should have full access in a couple of hours. And good luck with the repairs at Bloomers. You're my mom's favorite center."

Mom. I could be her mom, Aileen thought.

They closed with more small talk, including an admission from Aileen about how much Felicity looked like her daughter. A quick handshake and Aileen realized she had won her first battle.

Now to win the war, to solve a murder…

Chief Couch started with Rick. "How's he doing?" Aileen began a detailed update. Couch cut her off. "So he's fine, then?" Aileen saw his concern in spite of his choppy approach to chatting.

He slid a folder across his desk. The coroner's seal gleamed, official and ominous. The label had dates and names, but the one that mattered was in big letters, right under the seal: Ethan Lands Riley. Aileen tilted her head at the unusual middle name.

She scanned the report, page by page, reading each line. Unusual murder method. Left ear. Long, thin, round implement. Instantaneous death. No drugs, minimal alcohol. Body moved post-mortem. The data appendix didn't mean a lot to her.

Aileen stared at the ceiling, processing. Couch watched her like a predator, every muscle coiled, but he didn't attack, didn't speak.

"You own an ice pick?" he asked, changing the subject so fast Aileen had to pause.

"No," Aileen answered. "You're welcome to search my house."

Couch waved the suggestion away. "You're too smart to keep a murder weapon anyway." Aileen smiled at the backhand compliment.

Couch asked if Aileen might like to give him some information. He didn't wait for her answer. His interrogation style was pure chaos. Questions fired at the walls, the ceiling, bouncing around the room. Aileen tried answering. Couch ignored her responses, moving rapid-fire from one theory to another faster than she could follow.

She went silent, waiting.

Couch leaned forward, squinting. "You're clear," he announced. "Someone who takes care of Rick like you do couldn't be a murderer. And, uhh, I'm sorry I doubted you earlier." Couch's big ears were red around the edges.

Heat rose to Aileen's cheeks. Of course she was clear; she'd known it all along.

Without warning, Couch stood and reached across his messy desk to shake her hand. "That does it. I know who the killer is. You helped." Two bounces and he cleared the station's entrance.

He sped off, lights flashing and siren blaring, leaving Aileen stunned in his empty office.

Aileen called Bloomers from her car, and Verona answered. Aileen complimented Verona on the smooth intro to Bloomers that she gave on the phone. "Who's there today?" Aileen asked, surprised to find Jessie and Darwin were present. She knew Garrett had opened, so that made five for lunch. Maybe enough food for ten then, given Aileen's hunger and the known bottomless pits that teenagers could be at midday.

"What do you all want for lunch? I'm buying."

Verona yelled into the back and an eruption of ideas could be heard, no two the same. Aileen sighed and said she'd make it a surprise then, and yes, she remembered that Darwin had a shellfish allergy and Jessie didn't like hot dogs.

Aileen arrived with two massive buckets of Bullitt Chicken and a large sack of sides, earning applause from her troupe. Verona said she would take the credit, which brought a round of boos.

Lunch became an impromptu strategy session. Darwin, true to form, started mapping out more possible murder suspects while Garrett and Jessie cleaned up.

"Couch cleared me as a suspect," Aileen mentioned. Darwin muttered something about Andy being the one who should be worried, earning a swift punch in the shoulder from Verona. He feigned injury, though his smile gave him away. Then he remembered Aileen's real injury and apologized. Aileen smiled and waved him off.

When Aileen mentioned Rick's odd mumblings about Trey and Ryan, Jessie identified Trey Spalding as the Boucherons' chauffeur. Darwin's research antenna went up. He dug through the corners of the Web. When he found little information on his first look, he became more determined to dig deeper.

The crew chattered about Ryan next, missing for some days. Nobody had a clue where she was, but she'd been out of classes, unexcused.

"Why would Rick mention them?" Jessie wondered. Verona shrugged. "Probably the concussion."

The teens' casual collaboration impressed Aileen. Garrett suggested adding Marshall Boucheron and Quentin the butler to their suspect list. Darwin had already done so, but noted Tristan was off the list; currently in Cambodia, confirmed. They kicked the new suspect Marshall around and then struck him from the list. Bedridden invalids seldom commit murder, Cheryl suggested.

Later, while inventorying supplies with Jessie, Aileen shared her bank loan triumph as they moved items and built the list.

"Why tell me?" Jessie asked.

"I've just got to tell someone or I'll burst," Aileen exclaimed. "And I know you can be trusted."

Jessie smiled. "Thanks, Mrs. B, I try not to gossip. Not like Verona sometimes. But she's learning."

When Garrett and Darwin approached about taking off a bit early, Aileen knew something was up. Their shy confession, that they were going to find Gloriano, made her smile.

She shooed them out and returned to her ordering, already planning that new coffee pot.

✧ ◫ ✧ ◫ ✧

Darwin approached the auto shop's back lot like he expected trouble, hands visible. Gloriano lounged against the wall, cigarette pinched between two fingers. Darwin knew he'd be there, even with school out for the day. If he was on the grounds, he'd be there.

"What's up, *Hombrecito?*" Gloriano sneered. "Want a cig? Or maybe a wedgie?"

His laugh was harsh. Darwin's nervous chuckle matched it.

"Heard you were gonna work at Bloomers last summer," Darwin said.

Gloriano's face hardened. "Nah. Wanted to ride with my gang. Uncle tried getting me that job, but I don't do dirt and flowers. And that Brannigan *mujer?*" He spat on the ground.

Garrett emerged from around the corner, tipping his hat. Gloriano tensed, looking skittish.

"We just want to talk," Darwin said. "If Garrett starts something, I'll handle him." That got a laugh from Garrett and a snigger from Gloriano.

"Not afraid of some *vaquero falso*," Gloriano muttered, but his eyes darted around, looking for danger.

Darwin asked if he'd heard about what happened to Ethan. "Too bad," Gloriano said. "That *idiota* sure knew how to crack a car. I hoped to learn from him. How did you know Ethan, '*Cito*?" Gloriano's voice came harsh, overflowing with suspicion.

"I saw him with you Monday," Darwin offered. "I asked around and somebody recognized him. From years ago. Said he was called Ethan, they didn't know his last name."

"Yeah, nobody knows," Gloriano responded.

Darwin asked if he might have any idea who did Ethan in. Gloriano's answer was wary, hesitant. "Wasn't Paco's gang," he allowed. "Though they probably beat up that kid last night." He lit another cigarette, his face revealing he'd said too much.

Garrett's question caught him off guard. "You really like this gang stuff?"

"Hell yeah," Gloriano started, standing up straight. Then hesitated, slumping. "Some of it's bad. People get hurt."

Darwin pressed about consequences. Gloriano puffed on his cigarette, closed switchblade spinning between the fingers of his right hand.

"Bloomers might be a safe place," Garrett said. "If you need it."

As they walked away, Darwin called back, "Hey, maybe I'll take that cigarette next time."

Gloriano's laugh followed them. "Stick to wedgies, '*Cito*."

Marlene Niedermayer arrived at 4:15, her sensible tweed jacket pressed, reading glasses perched atop bright red hair. She wandered through the greenhouse section where the high school volunteers worked, inspecting their efforts.

"This vandalism," she said, stopping near a tray of spring seedlings, "it must be that homeless person. Scruffy, isn't it? Always hanging around town."

Aileen continued to repot a delicate, fragrant orchid. Her hands never stopped moving as she responded. "Marlene, we can't just assume. Every person deserves a fair assessment."

Marlene huffed. "In my two years of teaching, I've learned how to spot trouble."

"And in my years running Bloomers, I've learned people are more complex than they appear," Aileen countered.

Marlene nodded with no real conviction, bought a small plant for her desk, and left.

Henry Pettigrew walked in next. The new accountant in town, his crisp blue shirt starched, yellow polka-dot tie straight. He adjusted his wire-rimmed glasses and looked around Bloomers with a professional's critical eye. Aileen knew Henry had gone to Keating High, and from there to Stephen F. Austin for his accounting business degree. He might even know some of the teen brigade from school.

"Teen hoodlums," he declared as he placed the small, brightly-colored ceramic pot and Chinese money plant by the register. "Probably came from Tyler. Or maybe Jasper. Those areas have deep economic challenges." He fumbled with the word, clearly uncomfortable.

Aileen adjusted a display of spring bulbs. She stepped over to the register to clear Henry's tab. "Economic challenges aren't the same as criminal intent, Henry."

He nodded. "My folks, they weren't well off. Some of the things I heard in the neighborhood, they were scary." He handed over his credit card. Then he brightened.

"I could help," he offered. "With the accounting. After the damage. *Pro bono.*" He smiled, trying to hide his desperation. Aileen didn't commit, but said she'd visit after Easter and see what he could do for Bloomers.

Kyle Ferguson burst through the door, all firefighter muscle and barely contained energy. He'd changed from his shift uniform into tight jeans and a worn leather jacket over a Pearl Jam t-shirt. His eyes were dark with anger. He ignored the way all the ladies shopping in Bloomers paused to stare.

"It's Val," he announced to no one in particular. "She's trouble."

Aileen raised an eyebrow. "Sounds like there's a story there."

Kyle's face reddened. "Bad date. Really bad date." Kyle took off to wander along the tools wall, choosing a small grubbing hoe he probably didn't need. Aileen smiled as she rang up Kyle's purchase.

Andy Burrell and Fagan Sertsma arrived together, a Frank and Ernest study in contrasts. Andy, taller and with a slight paunch under his sports coat, moved in slow steps between plant displays. Fagan, shorter and thin, carried two large hanging baskets of Easter lilies to the front.

"The Boucherons," Fagan muttered, leaning close to Aileen. "Too much money. Always trouble."

"I wouldn't mind having some of that 'too much money,'" Aileen offered. "Wouldn't make me a criminal." Fagan scanned around Bloomers, noting how much progress had been made since the attack, and all the work that was still ahead.

"Yeah, well. I guess money really isn't the root of all evil." He chuckled as he realized his pun.

Aileen laughed. "No, it's love of money, Fagan. I don't want to marry it, just date some. For a while."

The ancient credit card reader chose that moment to balk, and Aileen wanted to slap some sense into that decrepit hunk of cantankerous electronics. She sighed, remembering her pledge to have Rick figure out the technical refresh for Bloomers. Rick; she'd run directly from the store to the hospital, as soon as she could close.

Andy shook his head as he waited out the balky register. "Outsiders," he said. "Not our kind of people. Not our kind of problem either, but they're making it ours."

"And our kind of problem is," Aileen challenged. She saw that he was buying the largest number of small flowers for replanting. Andy the confirmed bachelor, who likely didn't own any gardening tools. She understood what he was doing, and rang up the colorful collection, offering a ten percent volume discount. Andy declined, paid cash, and returned to his dispute with Fagan as they carried their winnings out of the store.

Aileen listened and watched. Sorting through theories seemed like sorting seedlings. Some might grow into something, most would wither. And sometimes the ones you thought were goners sprouted the strongest.

76

As the last customer left, she surveyed her shop, satisfied. Bloomers had survived another day, this one in style.

Twilight settled over Bloomers like indigo chiffon as Aileen gathered her scattered belongings. She clicked off the lights, checked locks, and stepped outside into the cooling evening. She hurried back to the checkout counter to grab the puzzle book she'd started that morning.

Chief Couch's cruiser rolled up, lights flashing and siren off, a careful courtesy to the neighborhood. His police equipment clinked and jangled with each step as he jogged over.

"Stopped by to thank you," Couch said, his manner brisk and businesslike. "It wasn't out of the way. Arrested Dakota. Couldn't have done it without you. Your input today."

He gave a quick, slightly comical salute and turned back to his cruiser.

Aileen stood motionless. Dakota? Arrested? Her input? What input? The dots in her mind refused to connect, spinning like loose compass needles.

Okay, she had admitted she was angry with Dakota for his small vandalism in Bloomers. From there to murderer, though; that was a big, big step.

She watched Couch drive away toward the jail, leaving behind confusion and unanswered questions.

"Dakota?" she muttered to herself. "How in the world...?"

She knew what to do next. Rick would want to know. Maybe he was ready to get out.

As she hurried to her car, one thought repeated: Something wasn't right. This couldn't be right.

Chapter Eight

Aileen drove by the Henslee residence. Darwin waited on the lower step of the porch, absorbed in his laptop. Aileen tooted her horn and waved. Darwin closed and stowed his computer and jogged down the path to the street, his big computer bag slung sloppily over his right shoulder.

"Good morning, Mrs. Brannigan," Darwin said.

"Are your parents okay with you coming out so early?" Aileen asked.

"No worries, they're already off to the lake for some boating. Makes me seasick just thinking about it."

"I heard your grandmothers were in town."

"Yeah," Darwin said, with less enthusiasm than Aileen expected. He wiggled against the seatbelt. "They left last night. Grandmother Irene is going to California, to the Jet Propulsion Lab."

"She's consulting there?" Aileen asked as they made the corner onto Maple. That didn't make sense, Aileen knew Irene wasn't an engineer.

"Not this time. She's meeting Doctor Gramps there. Something to do with some rocket motor." Darwin knew the details, but didn't want to bore Aileen.

"And Granma Bea? I was glad to see her Thursday at the shop."

"Yeah, she's sorry your business got hurt so bad. And your arm. She put the gnome in the back garden." Darwin didn't want to tell Aileen about all the tests he'd been subjected to this past week. He wanted to focus on solving the attacks and Ethan's murder.

At Bloomers, Aileen moved through her practiced opening pattern while Darwin ran to the break room. Once Aileen was satisfied that the shop was ready for customers she hurried to the back to start the coffee.

79

To her delight, the new coffee pot had arrived and Darwin had the brew gurgling. He had reassembled the shipping box, which now stood on the floor next to the drinks station, waiting to be stowed or recycled.

"You washed the pot out, yes?" she asked Darwin.

He stopped laying out snack supplies. "Oh shoot, I forgot," he admitted. "Does it matter?"

"A new coffeemaker might have contamination from manufacturing and logistics," Aileen said. She knew Darwin preferred bigger words. "But hey, companies are also not in the habit of poisoning their customers. At least not for very long," she finished.

Aileen poured a full travel mug's worth of the wonderful-smelling elixir, noting with satisfaction that this shiny Black & Decker had a "steal a cup" function so she could get her fix right away. Larger capacity than the old one too.

"What happened to the old machine?" Aileen asked.

"Went to the pet shelter," Darwin said as he opened his laptop and settled in. "I wanted to junk it, but Jessie said the pet shelter had a local post on Facebook asking for a donated maker. Garrett dropped it off on his way home yesterday."

Aileen hoped it would work for the shelter's volunteer crew, at least for a little while. She marveled at the way her misfits were working together so well. She chuckled.

Darwin looked up. "What?" he demanded.

"Oh, nothing. I figure I better find something useful to do around here or you youngsters will take over and make me stay home."

Darwin considered her statement. "You wouldn't like to stay home and play on your computer?"

"Haven't got one," she replied. "Only my phone. And it's old." More electronics challenges. Rick better get back here soon.

Darwin returned to his laptop, fingers dancing across the keyboard. Aileen stared into her coffee, thoughts churning.

Rick was improving, yes, and that was good. His color was back, and he was eating and wanting more. The bruises were fading, and no bones were broken. Youth's resilience, she mused. He couldn't remember much of the attack and she'd chosen not to remind him. Some memories were better left buried, at least for now.

Dakota's arrest still gnawed at her. Something didn't add up. Couch was being an idiot, and somebody needed to shake him.

"Call one of the others to come help you here," she told Darwin. "I'm going to the police station." Darwin nodded and touched more controls on his laptop.

When Aileen strode into the main room of the station, Delilah greeted her with her perpetual cheer. "Coffee?" she asked. "No snacks, though. Chief forgot to stop by Doughnut Stop Believin'. Oh, he's on the phone, you'll have to wait a bit."

Over police station coffee, probably no better than the Navy's cuppa Joe, Aileen probed Delilah for information. What did Chief Couch think he had on Dakota? Each detail fueled her growing anger.

When Couch hung up his phone call, Aileen stormed into his office. He jumped up from his desk and backed into the far corner, Adam's apple bobbing, unsure whether to call for help or brace for impact.

Aileen heard Delilah giggle, clearly entertained. Let her watch the floor show, Aileen thought. Maybe she'd learn something.

"Dakota couldn't have done this murder," Aileen declared. Her list was precise, methodical. Couch nodded vigorously, his agreement almost comical.

"Why the change of heart?" he asked. "You said he was the one."

"I never said Dakota was the murderer. You misunderstood." Aileen's anger grew with each mistake. "I bet you thought I accused Val Boucheron too."

"But what about —" Couch tried. Aileen cut him off with a harsh monotone, blowing up each detail.

Couch deflated, his circumstantial evidence destroyed under her outraged logic.

"How can you defend someone who threatened you?" he challenged, trying to crawl out from under the withering barrage.

Aileen paused. Couch had surfaced a new perspective she hadn't considered.

In her anger and frustration, it took a moment for her to find her voice. "Because what's right is right and everybody deserves a chance!" she yelled, stomping out and barely acknowledging Delilah.

Darwin would be waiting. The day was just beginning. Maybe it would be long enough for her to recollect her composure.

As soon as Aileen cleared the parking lot, Darwin called the team together in Bloomers' break room. They were assembled within minutes. Garrett slouched in a chair, Jessie perched on a stool, Verona leaned against a bench, and Cheryl on the corner of the table, fiddling with her notebook. The empty space where Rick usually sat felt conspicuous.

"No answer at the Ruggle residence. Again," Darwin reported, his fingers already mapping connections on their suspect board.

Jessie traced potential links with a red marker. "We're missing something. These connections aren't clear."

"Evidence," Darwin said. "Even small pieces matter. Circumstantial evidence can be the thread that unravels the entire mystery. How do we get some?"

Garrett's eyes drifted to the window. Gloriano stood outside, cigarette dangling, looking both tough and uncertain. Something about the way he shifted his weight suggested he wanted to talk but was too proud to ask. Why was he here?

"I'll be right back," Garrett mumbled.

Outside, Gloriano tensed as Garrett approached. "What do you want, *vaquero?*"

Garrett paused at a safe distance, not wanting to alarm the young Latino again. "Want to help us think?" Garrett's tone was casual, inviting.

Gloriano took a defensive step back. "Help? Me? Hey, I know nothing. I'm not smart like all of you." He crushed out his cigarette and fished around in a pocket for another.

"Seriously. We could use a different perspective." Garrett's smile was genuine. "I mean it, I'll eat my hat if I'm lying."

The offer seemed to disarm Gloriano. His shoulders relaxed a bit.

"Save the cig for later," Garrett suggested. "It's no smoking in the store. There will be time later." Gloriano put his smoke away.

Gloriano followed Garrett inside, looking like he might flee at any moment. The team greeted him with surprising normalcy. Verona offered a pastry which Gloriano accepted with mumbled thanks, moving closer to the work table. They continued like Gloriano had always had a place with them.

Darwin explained their investigative approach. "We need to systematically eliminate suspects. Each theory needs testing."

Verona nodded. "Like the scientific method, eh? Hypothesis, evidence, conclusion."

"Let's start with Dakota," someone offered. They were off, simultaneously drawing and talking. At first Gloriano was confused, then he began to catch on.

As they went down their long list of possibles, each offered their idea for where to look for confirmation they could use. Gloriano stayed quiet, watching each team player as they spoke.

At the end of the list they had Val, Trey and Quentin. Darwin pointed out this was the only obvious cluster on the list.

"How about this? A night break-in at the Boucherons," Jessie suggested. "They seem to be in the middle of this, somehow."

Gloriano leaned forward. "I can show you how to do that. But I'm not going near the place." He leaned in further, voice dropping. "It's haunted by *Madre* Ursula's *espectro*."

The team exchanged looks. Darwin raised an eyebrow. "What's that last word?"

Gloriano smiled. Something he knew that they didn't. "Ghost, *'Cito*, her spirit. Bad to challenge that."

"Ah," Darwin said. "Hey, maybe someday you can teach me some of those cool Spanish words?"

"I can do that. I just won't teach you any swear words." Everybody laughed while Darwin blushed.

"Back on track," Darwin said, grasping for the vanishing tatters of his dignity.

"Old money families have *muchos secretos*, secrets," Gloriano whispered, getting a chorus of nods. "Trust me."

Movement outside the undamaged window of the shop caught Cheryl's attention. "The boss is coming!" She stage-whispered.

Instant pandemonium. Papers shuffled, boards hastily flipped. Gloriano panicked. "I can't be seen here, not by her!"

Garrett didn't ask why. He guided Gloriano through to the back of the greenhouse just as Aileen's footsteps approached the front. The remaining teens arranged themselves into composed innocence.

Aileen's suspicious gaze swept the room. Why so many of them here, now? Not a single tell betrayed their secret meeting.

"Everything okay?" she asked.

"Absolutely, certainly, for sure, why wouldn't they be?" they chorused, almost too quickly.

Aileen shrugged. She was a puzzler, not a diviner. She poured a cup of coffee from the new brew station. She saw that there were two boxes from Doughnut Stop Believin', and that the contents, whatever they had been, were all gone. She smiled.

✧ ◻ ✧ ◻ ✧

The plate glass truck arrived with a promise of big improvements. Four installers came in a separate truck full of tools. As the installers replaced large glass panels Aileen watched the teens clear paths, their movements coordinated and purposeful. The shop was healing, one pane at a time.

The gaudy cream and maroon Rolls Royce announced itself before it stopped; gleaming, ostentatious, a rolling statement of wealth. Trey helped Val out with a flourish, escorting her toward Bloomers like they were attending a state function.

Aileen drained her cup and glanced skyward. She rose and rolled her shoulders, hoping her invisible armor would absorb the slings and arrows about to come. This could NOT be a gardening visit.

Aileen tried anyway. "Easter flowers for the estate?" Aileen offered, professional and measured.

Val's laugh was sharp. "My gardeners handle such trivial matters."

The break room felt smaller with Val occupying its space. She positioned her martini glass as if it were a museum sculpture. Trey placed a cocktail shaker like a supporting prop in their elaborate performance. Trey stepped back a few feet, pretending that made him invisible.

"You got me into trouble with Chief Couch," Val began, her opening salvo pointed and resentful.

Aileen bought time to think by pouring a little more coffee and adding some fortifying sugar. The ritual of filling and stirring gave her scope to breathe, to calculate. Trey declined her offer, his eyes never leaving Val.

"Lemonade," Val proclaimed, tossing back her drink. Trey refilled without comment.

Aileen's skepticism was a tangible thing, hanging in the air between them. Val didn't show any impairment, but then well-practiced alcoholics seldom did, until they fell down.

Aileen sat, back straight, and the argument escalated. Val's accusations flew like knives, Aileen deflecting with calm, even words. When Val stood, it was a dramatic exit, all motion and performance. She actually flounced, Aileen marveled, something she had to have practiced in front of a mirror.

"You'll be sorry!" she shrieked as she reached the front sales area. "You'll pay for insulting a Boucheron, you and your, your little monkeys!"

The shop went silent. The glass installers paused along with the rest, witnesses to this small-town drama.

Aileen watched them leave, recognizing that this was far from over. As the Rolls smoothed away she decided she would hold a war-room session with her subversives later on, preparing for what might come. And maybe finding some way to turn the tables.

85

The glass installers packed up, their movements marking the day's end. Aileen signed the lead installer's work receipt and thanked them when they said they'd be back on Monday. The light in the front sales room was so much better, with late afternoon sunshine turning everything to brass and bronze and gold.

Aileen called out that Bloomers was closed, sending the teens scattering like a broken covey of west Texas quail. All except Jessie, who lingered with shy nervous energy.

"Need something?" Aileen asked. She'd never seen Jessie hesitate.

"Just a ride to Lendon's for my part-shift," Jessie mumbled. They gathered their belongings and Jessie waited in the car as Aileen checked all the locks.

Jessie was silent, squirming all through the short ride to Lendon's Full Service Fuel & Lube. Her usual cheeriness was replaced by muffled responses to Aileen's questions about her day.

At the gas station, Aileen said she would like a few gallons of regular. Could Jessie get that for her? Less than a minute later Jessie showed up after changing her good clothes into Lendon-standard work duds: Blue cambric shirt, worn blue denim overalls and a used ball cap. She'd pulled her ponytail out the back over the cap's closure.

While Jessie filled the tank and hurried through the service steps, her nervousness bubbled over. "I'm scared," she declared, her voice small.

Aileen listened, remembering Rick's brutal attack. "Scared of what?"

"All this... violence. Somebody even died. We're getting too close to something very dangerous." Jessie pushed a rag into the back pocket of her denim overalls and turned to leave, then turned back.

Jessie's next words came in a rush. "Darwin and Verona are planning something stupid. A break-in, I think. At Boucheron Manor. Maybe even tonight." Jessie looked guilty. "Please don't tell them I said anything. I couldn't take it if —" She ran out of sight, back where the tires were stored.

Aileen's breath caught. Darwin, sweet, brilliant Darwin, potentially walking into a trap? Verona, so young, so eager, and often terribly silly. The thought of them in danger tightened her chest with a maternal fury that surprised her.

She drove by Darwin's house: empty. Verona's phone went straight to voicemail.

Aileen's fingers gripped the steering wheel, her knuckles white. One wrong move could put these kids in real danger.

Just as she was thinking about calling the rest of the teens to track down the potential troublemakers, her phone rang.

The caller ID flickered. Ryan. Unexpected, explosive. And why now? Lord, why now?

Aileen's finger shook as she pushed talk.

The northwest corner of Silvergrove looked like hope had died years ago. Abandoned storefronts, rusted cars on cinder blocks, windows like blind eyes staring at Aileen's outsider vehicle. No strangers allowed, they whispered. She'd pulled over, hands pale on the steering wheel, Ryan's cryptic instructions echoing in her mind. Ten minutes felt like ten years.

A timid tap sounded on the rear window. Aileen's finger almost broke the unlock button. Ryan fell into the car, shouting "GO!" Aileen's tires screamed against asphalt, leaving nothing but a cloud of smoke behind.

Once Aileen was sure they were away from whatever frightened Ryan, she peeked in the rearview mirror. Ryan was unrecognizable. Dirty, with gaunt cheeks and haunted eyes, the fashion-forward teen replaced by someone who looked like she'd fought a war and scarcely survived.

"Take me to another location," Ryan mumbled. "I have an address. From a friend."

Aileen's response was immediate and absolute. "No way! We're going to my house." Ryan wailed "NO!" but Aileen had the controls. Fifteen minutes later they were surrounded by the quiet, groomed neighborhood that Aileen had once believed was Silvergrove.

Ryan refused to go in the house, shaking on the floor of the back seat. Aileen wrapped her in a blanket, half-carrying her inside. The shower became Ryan's sanctuary, water washing away more than dirt.

Aileen took the opportunity to inspect the contents of Ryan's bag. One change of clothes. No second pair of shoes. No underwear, even. Thankfully, no drugs.

Aileen fixed a simple, tummy-friendly meal while Ryan finished her shower. Ryan looked around as she came slowly into the dining room, drying her hair. She let out a small whimper and ran to the windows, closing the blinds. She devoured the food like she might never get to eat again, asking politely for more. Two large glasses of milk disappeared. Satisfied, Ryan sat back. Hints of the Ryan of a week ago were showing up, but the haunted look in her eyes warned Aileen that the carefree girl might never come back. She prayed the girl's spirit hadn't died in the past week.

Aileen waited while Ryan rested, thinking, rubbing her damp locks. Without warning, the story began to tumble out, so fast that Aileen had to hug Ryan to slow her down.

Wednesday night, after word of Ethan's murder had spread through the town, Ryan had gone to the Boucheron estate. She had confronted Trey, saying she wanted out: No more drug mule activities, no more selling for him. Trey had exploded in anger and grabbed her from the back in a tight grip, yelling that he would rather have Quentin sell her than let her quit now. She was the best mule he ever had and he wasn't letting her go. The threat of being sold by Quentin kicked Ryan's self-preservation into overdrive, and she had instinctively used the self-defense moves she'd learned at camp the summer before.

She had twisted around enough to get a solid knee into Trey where it did the most good. When Trey wheezed and bent over, Ryan pulled free and gave him an even harder kick, right on target. Trey had folded up, howling in pain. Ryan had grabbed her bag and run all the way down the long drive.

Aileen asked a couple of questions during this flood of tormented words.

Ryan then explained how she had gotten a ride home from a kind stranger, packed some things and left. She knew where there was a hidey-hole, far from her house.

Her friend, the one with the hideout, turned out to be Scruffy. He often slept in the office area of the abandoned Piggly Wiggly and she had walked the six miles there, in the dark. Scruffy helped her get settled with some musty warm blankets and food, mostly Vienna sausages and beer. Then he had left.

"He was like a guardian angel," Ryan said in a wondering whisper. "He told me he patrolled like he used to, in Afghanistan. But that he hadn't had to kill anybody to protect me. Not this time." Ryan tried out a small laugh that turned into a stifled sob.

Aileen listened. No judgment. Just presence. When Ryan ran out of story, Aileen hugged her again, long and hard, ignoring the soft weeping against her shoulder.

After Ryan's energy subsided and the tears slowed, Aileen suggested they go upstairs and watch some TV or something. Ryan readily agreed, ashamed of her display. Before the first commercial, exhaustion claimed the young woman. Within moments of settling in front of the television Ryan was fast asleep, the oblivion of one who hadn't slept well in days.

Aileen carried her to the guest room, covered her and went downstairs to her own bed. She forgot, entirely, that Darwin and Verona were planning anything at all.

Chapter Nine

The breakfast nook felt like a fortress under siege. The blinds were drawn tight, spring sunlight seeping through around the edges. Aileen's coffee cooled as her thoughts churned.

Two weeks without church. Two weeks of constant tension. The beautiful Texas spring was happening just outside her window, and she was trapped inside her own house. Ryan's presence was a comfort and a constraint, her gratitude wrestling with a growing sense of restlessness.

Where were Darwin and Verona? Had they attempted that ridiculous break-in? She started more than once to call the police station and check if they had two truant teens. Her mind recoiled from the option of calling the morgue.

The phone rang under her hand. Gleason Memorial. Aileen's mind flooded with relief when she learned that Rick would be discharged between one and two. A burst of pure joy cut through her morning fog. Something was going right for once! She promised to be there at one o'clock sharp. She rejected the whisper in her mind that said she should have asked about Verona and Darwin.

Ryan emerged, looking more like the teen of old. More human. The haunted eyes remained, a reminder of recent trauma, but her movements were stronger. Breakfast became a ritual of recovery: large portions, inconsequential chatter and the slow rebuilding of regularity.

Another call came in. The caller ID showed "Police" this time. Aileen beseeched the heavens and answered. Delilah wanted to let Aileen know that Dakota's release was imminent, Chief's orders. They weren't going to charge him with murder, and since Aileen didn't want to press vandalism charges, he'd be free to go. Chief Couch said for them to all watch out, they didn't know what Dakota might do next. Aileen found the courage to ask after her wayward duo. No, nothing here, Delilah said. Aileen hung up before Delilah could ask why.

Aileen refused to let Dakota's impending freedom steal her moment. Rick was coming home to rest and heal. This would be his home while he recovered, for as long as he wished. Ryan was safe. The day might actually be turning. Take the wins, the gentle voice in her head whispered.

Spring kept on outside, warm and indifferent to the humans and their dramas.

Delilah's fingers moved through the release paperwork, each stapled document a testament to bureaucratic precision. Dakota sat, watching. His personal effects, a wallet, a cheap watch, some loose change, looked as worn and indifferent as he did.

"You're free to go," she said, her tone even but edged with something else. Disappointment? Resignation?

Chief Couch loomed, a human thundercloud. "Listen, kid. One more mistake and you're back here so fast your head will spin. Maybe you should clean off. Don't even think about jaywalking."

Dakota's smirk never wavered. "Yes, sir," he drawled, the words dripping with mockery.

"You're lucky Aileen isn't pressing charges," Couch growled. His massive hands clenched and unclenched.

As Dakota walked out, he turned and waved. "I'll be sure to take care of that, Chief," he said, a sly promise hanging in the words.

Delilah's hand on Couch's arm prevented him from crossing the room, though barely.

Outside, Dakota strolled past churchgoers, chuckling to himself. Palm Sunday. How perfectly ironic.

Aileen could see Ryan's nerves jangling like broken wind chimes. The doorbell's single tone sent her fluttering up the stairs, a sparrow escaping a hawk's shadow.

Aileen peered through the peephole. Dakota. Smiling. Waving at neighbors like a politician on parade.

She could ignore him, she thought. Dakota wasn't the type to fade away, though. She chuffed and unlocked the door.

"You're out!" she said, opening the door with manufactured brightness.

Dakota's smile didn't reach his eyes. "Stopped by to thank you. For helping yesterday."

"Neighborly thing," Aileen responded, flat and measured.

"Neighborly? Like breaking your pot?" A test. A probe.

Aileen refused the bait. Her silence hung between them, a weapon more precise and sharp than words.

Dakota's smile flickered, faded, was gone. "I've got advice," he said. "Leave town. Or my cousin Ethan might not be the only fresh grave up the hill."

"Got a business to run," she answered. "Not going anywhere."

"Ready for round two?" The smug smirk was back, with something more underneath.

His laugh echoed down the street, scattering churchgoers like startled pigeons.

Aileen stood behind her closed door, hands on her hips, trying to fathom what that was really all about. The hall clock chimed once, and Aileen remembered she had an appointment at Gleason Memorial Hospital to collect Rick. And she was late, as of Right Now.

She grabbed her handbag and yelled up the stairs: "Ryan, I have to go out. Honey, come lock the door. I won't be long." Aileen rushed out too fast to hear if Ryan was coming down the stairs.

A finance officer greeted Aileen and escorted her to a small, private office just off the foyer. The paperwork to gain Rick his freedom from Gleason Memorial felt like signing a nonaggression treaty. Aileen worked through each form, grateful for her business insurance and having the financial bandwidth to cover unexpected expenses. Her fingers moved through the papers without pause, a far cry from the uncertainty of previous weeks. She acknowledged the change; welcomed it.

When Rick appeared, wheelchair-bound and protesting, Aileen's heart lifted. "I can walk!" he complained to the nurse, who remained implacably professional. Hospital policy, she said. Her tone brooked no argument.

Rick's grumble transformed into a broad smile once he saw Aileen. He tried to stand, reaching for her, but the nurse's firm hand kept him seated. "Not so fast, cowboy," she said. "You two can huggie-kissie after you're out of my sight!" Aileen saw the twinkle in the nurse's eye.

"You look good" was all she could squeeze out without choking up.

Rick winced a couple of times as he settled into the passenger's seat and buckled in. "You hungry?" Aileen asked, desperate for something safe to talk about. What a silly question, she thought. He's a teen boy and fresh out of the hospital. He must be starving. "Well, what would you like?" she added.

Willard's Best BBQ was their first stop. Smoky aromas filled the car, promising comfort and renewal. "We're going to love this," Aileen said, and Rick nodded. He made no comment about how big the bag was.

At home, the reunion between Rick and Ryan was pure warmth. They hugged and then settled into careful questions.

"How are you doing?" Rick asked Ryan. "Where have you been?"

Aileen interrupted. "Let's eat first. Lemonade's ready."

Over lunch, stories unfolded. Ryan detailed her escape from Trey, her time with Scruffy, her days of abject terror that Trey or his lackeys might find her. Rick listened, occasionally wincing. "Did Trey really say something about selling you?" Rick asked, nearly in shock.

Ryan only nodded, unable to repeat the threat, even days later. Rick saw how distressed she was and relented.

"You need to give me the details about your fight," Ryan said, changing the subject.

Rick let out a big sigh and took another bite of his brisket sandwich. "Wasn't much of a fight, just a couple of hits," he allowed. "They hit me, I hit the ground. I was looking at messages on my phone rather than paying attention." He paused, inspecting Ryan for clues.

He put his sandwich down. "You know, we always tell the girls not to victimize themselves. Then we go and let it happen to us."

Aileen reached behind to the counter. She handed Rick his phone. "Manville found it and gave it to me. He's the one who raised the alarm," Aileen said. She'd never again say anything about Manville being a nosy old busybody.

Ryan and Aileen smiled together. "Give me more," Ryan said.

"After the first few punches I don't really remember," Rick said. "At least nothing's broken," he said, embarrassed. "Bruised ribs, and this shoulder will take a while to feel right. Should've been more careful. I bet I could've outrun those guys."

Aileen caught Ryan's eye. Male bravado was universal. Rick's status as a soccer star didn't help.

"The Koalas made the finals in soccer," Ryan said. "They won't play until next Wednesday, though. Holidays. You going to play?"

Rick shook his head, his mouth full of potato salad. He swallowed. "Nah, I won't be fit. Coach Anderson stopped by yesterday and asked, but I said he should give Laurent more field time. No way I'll be ready, even if the game's three weeks from now."

"Sorry," Ryan whispered. She knew how much the game meant to him. Finals too.

After lunch, collective exhaustion settled across the happily-full trio. They napped, reconvening in the afternoon with renewed energy.

"We need to solve this," Rick said. "Silvergrove deserves better than an unsolved murder and random vandalism. And threats of more violence." Rick stared at Aileen.

They parsed through suspects. Val Boucheron. Trey. Quentin. As before, each name carried potential, with no clear resolution. And there were still the minor names on the sheet Darwin had left with Aileen. Which brought Darwin back to her thoughts. Annoyance warred with dread about her youngest teens.

"I think we need to focus on these three," Ryan said. "Trey attacked me, he mentioned Quentin, and Val's been acting richer than creosote. It's gotta be one of them."

"Croesus," Rick said. "It's King Croesus of Lydia who was filthy rich. Creosote's sticky and smells bad."

Ryan stuck out her tongue. "Now you sound like Darwin. And 'sticky and smells bad' could describe you, after a soccer game. Maybe your new nickname is 'Creosote'?"

Rick stuck out his tongue in return. They all laughed.

"Speaking of our resident Einstein, where is Darwin? I thought he'd be here by now."

"I haven't told the rest of the team that you're out yet," Aileen deflected. She didn't want Ryan or Rick to know that Darwin and Verona might be doing something stupidly dangerous. "Besides, I called Darwin yesterday, no answer. Maybe he went to the lake with his folks." She remained silent about Verona.

"That little puppy? He hates water. He can get seasick watching a half-full gallon bucket." Rick snorted at Ryan's image.

He took over the conversation. "So if it's really one of the three up at the Boucheron place, how do we whittle it down to one? And then prove it?"

"We need a trap," Ryan said. "We need to catch whoever did this."

Rick nodded. The investigative spirit burned in his eyes. They batted ideas around for another quarter hour, thinking hard about what might work for each suspect. They agreed that they couldn't set three traps, and they couldn't choose any one without more information.

As afternoon light softened, they dispersed. Rick moved to the game room sofa for more napping. Ryan went to the guest bedroom, phone in hand, and closed the door. Aileen moved to the back porch, a cold soda and gathering sunset her only companions.

The day felt like a pause. A deep breath before a run. A moment of calm before something inevitable approached. Blue sky, just before thunder.

✧   ⌑   ✧   ⌑   ✧

Gloriano's crash course in amateur burglary hadn't exactly transformed Darwin and Verona into master criminals. Their determination made up the difference. They had all the equipment: Flash drives, SSD, lockpicks, sterile sample collecting materials and more.

They were all in black, one of the hardest parts of the preparation. Gloriano's *Tio* had been told a lie, that they were going to go to a costume party as ninjas, and he had driven them to Lufkin and helped them pick out clothes.

Gloriano helped them up onto the back fence of the estate, waved and left. He would wait a while down by the road, and if they didn't show he planned to leave and maybe call the cops. He smiled at the duo, but he wondered if they wouldn't be captured. Or worse.

"Safety pin," Darwin muttered, feeling the draft from the rip in his pants. "Totally professional."

Verona rolled her eyes. "Stealth master." She expertly pinned the slice shut, then put her gloves back on.

The Boucheron Manor house loomed like a sleeping dragon. They stood at the back of Ursula's abandoned studio, catching their breath and ramping up their courage. The unlocked back door into the kitchen welcomed them like a surprise invitation to a party. Darwin's digital toolkit and evidence collection gear clinked in his backpack. One wrong move and they'd be caught faster than a stray cat at a dog show.

"Red lights," Verona whispered. "Like we're in some low-budget spy movie."

They had no trouble finding the main office. It had artifacts on the walls and tables, in display cases and on the desk. Darwin's computer raid finished in minutes. His high-speed SSD drive sucked up data files at a steady, rapid clip. While the drive drained the desk machine Darwin and Verona went through all the drawers. They found a cell phone and flash drives tucked away. "Burner phone, I bet," Darwin whispered.

"Can we leave now?" Verona hissed. Darwin shook his head. They needed to find physical evidence of a violent death, murder by ice pick or similar. The kitchen had a small one, rusty; not the murder weapon.

They went up the stairs. The night nurse tending to Marshall became their first near-disaster. They squeezed into a space so tight that breathing seemed optional. She walked by, oblivious.

Then the vase got in the way. Verona jiggled the small hall table and the piece of Oriental art wobbled and fell.

Darwin's dive was part shinobi, part desperate teenager. Catching the expensive porcelain mid-fall, he looked like a freeze-frame from an action movie. He handled the vase as if breathing migh break it, and moved to put the it back. His knee bumped the table, which fell, tripping him. The vase followed and was art no more, just momentary noise and porcelain shards.

"Run!" Verona hissed.

The butler's pantry became their sanctuary. Darwin flipped the latch just as footsteps approached. They sat, hearts pounding, breath held, listening to the door handle jiggle.

"If we die," Darwin whispered as the footsteps retreated, "I'm blaming Gloriano."

Verona moved around on her hands and knees, shining her dim red flashlight everywhere. She found two blood drops. "Do they prep meat in here?" she whispered. Darwin said he didn't think so, handing her sample collection wipes and vials. "Could this really be the place?"

Darwin showed her two ice picks. He packed them up and continued ransacking drawers and shelves. He found a bloody towel, neatly folded, on the bottom of the stack of towels. Evidence collection turned treasure hunt.

After a long wait with no sounds in the hall, they returned to the kitchen. The back door was now locked. The security alarm's shriek threatened to wake the dead.

The two youngsters sprinted for their lives.

They tossed their packs over the fence, then climbed. Darwin ripped his pants again, opening the backside like trapdoor long-handles. Verona's ankle became a liability when she dismounted badly. She had to hold onto Darwin's shoulder and hop along on one foot. Gloriano was long gone.

Two long miles later the duo stopped. Darwin called the only person he trusted at a time like this.

When Aileen arrived, her face was a mixture of fury, concern, and disbelief.

"You two," she said, "are going to be the death of me." They held up their packs in victory.

Chapter Ten

Bloomers looked like a military war room rather than a flower shop. Exhaustion hung in the air, draping itself over Aileen, Darwin, and Verona. The others were all fresh from a restful weekend. The contrast actually hurt Aileen's eyes.

"We're all cutting school," Aileen muttered, a mix of maternal worry and criminal conspiracy dancing in her eyes. "I could go to jail for this."

The teens laughed and kept working. Darwin hunched over his laptop, financial files scrolling like incomprehensible morse code. "Money is weird," he announced. "These numbers make zero sense." He sat back in resignation. "I think the answer is in here, somewhere."

Aileen's pragmatic brain kicked in. "I know someone who can help," she said as she dialed. A cheery "Good Morning, Northside Bank, how may I direct your call?" poured from the new speakerphone in the center of the massive flower display table that now served as investigator's workspace. "Patrick Hamilton, please." A short pause and Patrick's voice boomed.

"Good morning Aileen! Everything going well at Bloomers?" Aileen said repairs were moving along, and she had a request.

"I have some financial documents here I don't understand. I wondered if you could loan me your analyst, Felicity, to help me out?" Aileen showed crossed fingers to the silent team. "She was so courteous the other day, and so efficient."

Hamilton agreed and asked when Felicity could stop by. Aileen grimaced at the thought of more white lies. "Uhh, Patrick, to tell the truth, I'm in a time bind. Can she come now?" The whole team put up crossed fingers. Hamilton put Aileen on hold. Low-fidelity elevator music crackling from the phone. He came back quickly and said Felicity was on her way. Aileen thanked him and signed off. The whole team swapped high-fives.

Aileen sensed Felicity's reluctance when she saw the teens around the table. "Felicity, this is my team of investigators. Would you be willing to hold a secret for a bit?"

She nodded as she considered.

"Darwin here has a cache of financial information he doesn't understand." Felicity squinted at the youngest member of the group, who waved his fingers in response. "If you don't ask about how he got it, he won't have to lie to you."

Without a word, Felicity opened her laptop next to Darwin's. He tossed her a web link and they were connected. Data flooded both screens while Aileen watched over their shoulders.

The flow froze at her touch of a key. Felicity moved the data up and down, slowly, then opened a suite of analytical tools. "This is going to take a while," she cautioned.

Darwin tapped an instruction. "Here's a cluster you can use. It's one experimental supercomputer and several servers. It's the best I can do," he admitted. Felicity looked like she might regret all this.

Spreadsheets and summaries burned up the airwaves between Silvergrove and Stephen F. Austin University. Felicity started to ask how, and Aileen raised a finger. "Please, you really don't want to know." Darwin's head bobbed.

While the analysts worked, Garrett sidled up next to Aileen. "Verona gave me these." He showed the illicit evidence bags. "I need to take them to a buddy of mine over in Milam, at a private crime lab. I called, he's not busy and could start today, now."

Aileen nodded assent without looking away from the scrolling data, hypnotized. When Garrett didn't move, she looked at him.

"Sorry, ma'am," Garrett said. 'Can I borrow a few bucks? Angel's out of gas." A couple of minutes later and ten dollars lighter, Aileen watched Garrett speed away. Angel? Only a wannabe Garth Brooks would name his car that.

"Aha!" Felicity leans forward. "Look here, Darwin! Got'em, by golly," she said. Aileen had to smile at Felicity's swearing style, so much like her own. "Boucheron accounts. Shoot, there are some at our bank! Is this illegal?"

Aileen held a finger across her lips, then pretended to zip her mouth shut. The teens mirrored her motions, failing to hide bright smiles.

Felicity sent an AI-generated composite analysis and closed her laptop. She stood and Aileen thanked her. "If Chief Couch asks, I was never here."

The teens all applauded Felicity's skills and her acceptance of inclusion.

"So we know about the money flows. And guess what?" Aileen asked the assembled class.

Expectant faces waited. "Val has complete control of the family finances, I suspect. She must have full power of attorney over Marshall at this point."

Darwin pressed a few keys, then looked up, nodding assent. Aileen could see her jail years piling up with each admission. Check that box, she thought. The suspects list shortened to one.

Aileen turned to the next step: Physical evidence. Which would be a while, she thought.

"If and when the forensic data comes back from Milam, how can we match it to the victim?"

Darwin didn't look away from his screen. "I have the coroner's report. It has a DNA profile in the appendix. They looked in the National Crimes Database to confirm Ethan's identity." Another box checked, more years added to Aileen's sentence. By now she didn't care. She'd take the fall for this quirky, brilliant team, even if she was never getting out.

Jessie storyboarded a scene to trap Val, all big gestures and fast talk. Theater was her favorite class, and this was a perfect exercise to show Mr. Ball. Only she couldn't, not yet. Maybe not ever.

Jessie looked up. "All we need is bait and we've got her."

After a moment of silence, the team yelled in unison: "Kyle!"

Aileen remembered the heat in Kyle's voice on Friday. She powered up the speakerphone and dialed the firehouse. Kyle wasn't there, so she called the lumber yard. When Kyle's baritone came on, the team listened in anticipation.

"Hi Kyle. I've got a big ask, involving Val."

Aileen heard Kyle grumble. "Yeah? I won't be sending her any flower telegrams," he continued.

"How would you like to get some back after your date the other evening?"

"I'd like that very much," Kyle agreed. "Do I get to play bill collector or something? I'd sure like to smash that mouthy chauffeur of hers in the face."

"Something like that," Aileen hedged. "Is there any way you can come to Bloomers and talk? Like, now?" All around the table, pairs of crossed fingers were waving.

"I'll go on break and be there in five," Kyle agreed, signing off.

The teens erupted. The trap was taking shape, one bizarre piece at a time.

✧ ◻ ✧ ◻ ✧

Kyle arrived in his shiny Ford truck. He stopped when he saw all the kids. "Flower arranging class?" he asked. Aileen laughed.

"Might be something like that, or maybe not."

The teens dragged him over to the storyboard and walked him through the plan. With each youngster chiming in regularly, the presentation became a rapid-fire mass of confusing steps and options.

Aileen interrupted. "What do you need Kyle to do, and when?" she directed. "One spokesman, one step at a time, in order."

"Call Val and arrange lunch someplace," Jessie suggested.

"Now?"

Nods of assent. Aileen thought they were rushing, but waited to hear their idea.

"Okay. Right back to Casa Sol. What better place to apologize than where the whole mess started?" It took less than three minutes and the date was set. Kyle left to get the sawdust off and dress up.

Ryan called Casa Sol and made the reservation. "Same table as before," she said. "It'll be ready when they get there."

Darwin said, "We need gear. I've got most of the pieces. Verona, can you go to Device Diva's and get these items?" Darwin's portable printer spat out a short list. "Hurry, we need to have them at Casa Sol in an hour."

"Done," Verona said, then stopped. "How can I pay?"

Aileen rolled her eyes. "I'll call and set up an account for Bloomers. Rick, when this is over, you and I are going to talk about a full equipment plan for the store." Rick nodded.

Ryan volunteered for microphone and camera placement. "I'll sweet-talk James," she insisted, "I left him a big enough tip on Saturday." Aileen protested about her safety. Ryan's Italian side broke through.

"Hey! I'm not a baby. Everybody else is taking risks. After I do what Darwin tells me I'll hide in the ladies' until it's all done."

Aileen squinted at Ryan, then nodded.

Each teen went to cover individual tasks. Time was short, but they believed.

Darwin settled into Aileen's car, headphones on. "Nobody notices a kid listening to music," he assured her.

Kyle arrived early at Casa Sol, somewhat overdressed for lunch anywhere else in Silvergrove. Ryan fitted his mic, watched out the window for a quick thumbs-up from Darwin, then disappeared into the powder room. The Rolls pulled up on schedule. Trey waited outside, annoyed that Val didn't want him with her.

As the appetizer disappeared, Kyle played his part. He was a gentleman, apologizing while Val consumed a large glass of some unpronounceable red wine. He even took a few careful sips.

The main course of surf-and-turf arrived, beautifully arranged on a platter that should have required two waiters to carry. "My favorite," Val exclaimed. "How did you know?"

"I guessed," Kyle lied. "Besides, it's mine too." Surely another lie didn't matter by now.

As the luxurious fare vanished, along with the rest of the bottle for Val, Kyle worked on his nerve.

"How did the Boucherons get their money?" he asked, watching Val's reaction.

Suspicion flickered in her eyes, her fork stuck somewhere between plate and lips. "Why do you want to know?"

Kyle nearly choked on his steak. "Just small talk. It's obvious you've got plenty."

Val settled back and told a tale of a poor Frenchman who made good, first as a young man in Lyon, and later in America. A practiced response.

Kyle steered the conversation to Ethan's murder. Mysterious. Intriguing. Val's wine glass never went empty; a second bottle suffered a severe dent.

Dessert arrived. The trap tightened.

"I watch lots of murder-mysteries," Kyle revealed, wiggling the hook. "I wish I knew where Ethan really was done in."

"The murder didn't happen at the cemetery," Val whispered, leaning close. "I know exactly where, how, and when."

Kyle stopped eating the dessert he didn't want and leaned in as well. "Give," he prompted.

Val swigged her wine, swaying a bit from its effects. "Well, mister firefighter hunk, it'll cost ya."

Kyle knew this was the moment. He didn't want to agree, but he remembered the busted date and the way the kids had looked at him at Bloomers that morning. He took the plunge.

"You're the one with the money," he teased, mischief creeping into his voice. He settled into the role now, finding it easier to mask sincerity behind playful banter.

She waved that off. "Piffle on money. I want you. At the manor this afternoon."

"Can't get off work," he resisted, trying to be authentic like Jessie had coached him.

"Double piffle. Who's your boss? I'll call him myself."

Kyle almost fell out of his chair. "Oh no, don't do that! I'll call, tell him I'm sick or something." He gulped wine he didn't want to cover his terror.

"So it's a deal?" Val pushed. Kyle breathed in and nodded, hiding behind the last fork of his dessert.

In Aileen's car, Darwin listened and made sure both recorders were going.

"Okay, your turn. You really know?" Kyle asked.

"Sure as you're the hottest lumber wrangler in Silvergrove," Val teased.

Darwin signaled. Aileen called Couch. He lurked near City Lake at Aileen's request.

The police cruiser's siren cut through the air, tires squealing to a halt. Officers swarmed Val before she could finish her sentence, drowning out Kyle's feeble protests. Trey stood as if cut from marble, watching in helpless confusion as handcuffs clicked shut around his charge's wrists and the officers led her away.

Aileen walked to her car where Darwin announced success to the teens via live chat. Just another day in Silvergrove, she thought. Though we need more like this one.

✧ ⌗ ✧ ⌗ ✧

The Milam crime lab's report came back quickly. That tech really must like Garrett's music, Aileen thought. She forwarded the data to Darwin. He called Aileen a couple of minutes later.

"The blood's a perfect match," Darwin said.

"How perfect?" Aileen asked. She had no idea how 'perfect' a match could be.

Darwin paused. "In this case, since that lab didn't have a primary refence sample, only the coroner's report, it's so-so. Maybe one chance in 170,000 that the match is a mistake. The odds of there being another person with the same DNA is much lower, though. Maybe one in 80 million."

That sure seemed like good numbers, but Aileen pressed for confirmation. "I have to be sure, Darwin, I'm going to present our case to Couch. What if Ethan had a twin?"

"Not possible," he said. "We have his birth records, since he has a criminal conviction."

"Good enough for me," she said. "I'm off to see the Chief."

"Hold on!" Darwin yelled. "There's more. One ice pick showed traces of human blood under the escutcheon, whatever that is. Not enough to build a full DNA profile, though. I'm sending documents to the printer at Bloomers."

Aileen gathered her printed evidence, papers curated and vetted by the teen investigators. Each page represented hours of work, careful analysis, a mosaic of clues piecing together a murder's hidden narrative.

Driving to the police station, she caught a glimpse of Gloriano. He looked different, in a blue polo shirt and charcoal slacks. A far cry from his usual street-worn appearance. She waved, he waved back. A fleeting moment of connection that disappeared quickly as her attention refocused on her mission.

Couch listened. Not with the dramatic skepticism she expected, but with a quiet, almost contemplative attention. A few questions, lots of listening. He sat, unmoving, at the end of Aileen's rational exposition.

"Do you really believe this?" he asked, leaning forward on his desk.

"I'd bet Bloomers on it," Aileen responded. With her offer, Aileen realized how much she trusted the team's work. A single toss, win or lose; these dice could only roll sevens.

He nodded. Not just an acknowledgment, but something deeper. A recognition.

"So would I," Couch said. "Not for the same reasons."

The cryptic response hung in the air between them.

Driving back, Aileen felt a surge of pride. Her team, these remarkable, unconventional sleuths, had pulled together something extraordinary. An ice cream celebration was definitely in order.

Bloomers and Rick waited, new computers to spec out. And the sweet taste of a case solved would last well past closing.

The blue glow of multiple monitors painted Darwin's face in harsh shadows. He should be sleeping, as tomorrow would be another long day at Bloomers, but something about Felicity's analysis gnawed at him. His brain churned between glee at trapping a murderer and his instincts that they had missed something important.

Felicity had done good work, he had to admit. Clean. Thorough. The money trail to Val was clear as crystal, which was exactly what chewed on him. In his limited experience, real financial crimes were messy, full of dead ends and false starts. This was too... perfect. Okay, he didn't have that much real-crime experience, but he'd read many mysteries that involved computers. He could binge on "Suits" all day.

Darwin cracked his knuckles and settled deeper into his desk chair. The quiet hum of his home-built server was comforting as he connected to the university cluster he'd been borrowing processing time from. What would Dr. Martinez think if she knew her prize computational array was being used to solve a murder? He checked in through the cluster's security system and pushed the financials over.

"Show me what everyone else missed," he muttered, diving into the Boucheron accounts. He focused on the 48 hours surrounding Ethan's death, scanning for anything Felicity might have dismissed as noise. There: a string of ATM withdrawals, relatively small amounts, spread across three bank locations. Curious. Maybe nothing. Better check.

Breaking the three banks' security systems took longer than he'd expected. These weren't the ancient watchdogs he usually encountered. Still, persistence paid off, and by 2 AM he was scrolling through camera footage synchronized to withdrawal timestamps.

The first video made him sit up straight. There was Val, yes, but she wasn't alone. A man Darwin didn't recognize stood close; too close for a stranger. They laughed about something, some intimate joke. Val playfully shoved the man's shoulder as she pocketed the cash.

Darwin checked the next video. Same man, same playful mood. And the next. His heart raced as he checked timestamps against the presumed timeline of Ethan's murder.

"No way," he whispered, double-checking his math. The last two withdrawals were well after Ethan's confirmed time of death. He watched the key videos a second time. Then a third. Val couldn't have killed him. She'd been too busy flirting with mystery man at ATMs across town.

Their entire case, all their careful deductions, collapsed like a house built on quicksand. One good shake was all it took. Darwin grabbed his phone, not caring about the late hour. Aileen answered on the fourth ring, her voice thick with sleep.

"Darwin? Dear, what's wrong?"

"Everything," he said, pulling up the video files to send her. "We got it all wrong, Mrs. B. Val didn't kill Ethan. She couldn't have. And I can prove it."

Chapter Eleven

Aileen stood in the dark at her kitchen window, still processing Darwin's revelations about Val. The coffee maker gurgled behind her; sleep was pointless now anyway. Through the window, her car sat in the driveway, a darker shape against the pre-dawn gray. She could use the time to figure out how to take Darwin's revelation to Couch. So much work turned to dust.

The first flash broke like lightning. The second brought a surge of heat that made her stumble back. Her car erupted into an inferno, flames clawing at the dark sky. The blast rattled her windows; somewhere down the block a dog began to howl.

She fumbled for her phone, fingers shaking as she dialed 911. That's when she saw dark figures moving across her front lawn. One stopped to plant something near her flower bed. Another made a throwing motion, and something heavy crashed through her front window. God no, not more fire! A rock, with paper, tied with string.

"Fire department, what is the nature of your emergency?"

Before Aileen could answer, her phone buzzed with an incoming text. Darwin: **GANG MEMBERS IN MY YARD. STAY INSIDE.**

Another text chirped in. Cheryl: **Someone's outside my house**

Then Verona: **help**

Jessie: **They're everywhere**

The dispatcher continued talking, but Aileen couldn't hear over her pounding heart. Movement caught her eye: someone walking up her driveway. Not skulking like the others, but striding purposefully. Flames illuminated Gloriano's face as he surveyed the burning car.

The dispatcher spoke louder, capturing Aileen's attention. She gave her address, and said to hurry. She gave a short, quivering laugh, the stress about the attack and relief that her house wasn't on fire whipsawing her nerves.

"Miss Aileen!" Gloriano called out. "*Señora* please, are you okay in there?"

She hesitated. Through the window, she saw more figures retreating into the shadows. One looked like they had a rifle, running behind the others. Gloriano stood alone in the firelight, hands raised to show they were empty.

"I saw them coming," he said. "I can help."

Her phone buzzed again. Rick, from upstairs, on the group chat: **All team homes hit. They know who we are. I'm calling Couch.**

The fire truck's sirens wailed in the distance as Aileen stared at Gloriano standing next to the flames. His face showed genuine concern, but how had he known? Why wasn't he afraid of the gang members who'd just marked every team member's home?

"*Doña* Brannigan?"

She took a deep breath and opened her door. The heat from her burning car hit her like a physical wall. Her fear turned to fury, hot as the car. "Start by telling me how you knew," she demanded.

Gloriano glanced over his shoulder at the retreating shadows. "That's... complicated."

Aileen's hand shook as she unlocked Bloomers' front door. The spare key felt wrong in her fingers. Everything felt wrong this morning, even the pretty spring sunrise. Rick was already inside, checking each greenhouse zone, his usual morning routine a lifeline of balance and regularity.

"Cameras are good," he called out, proud of the new security system installed the day before. "No damage here. Nothing missing that I can see."

She nodded, unable to find her voice. She still clutched her car insurance card in her other hand, edges crumpled from hours of worrying. The smell of smoke clung to her clothes.

The team filtered in through various entrances over the next fifteen minutes. Darwin showed first, his laptop bag clutched tight, dark circles under his eyes. Jessie and Verona arrived together through the back greenhouse, having walked the long way around to avoid main streets. Cheryl slipped in through the loading area, brushing leaves off her shoulder. Garrett was last, still watching the street through narrowed eyes as he closed and locked the front door.

Nobody spoke until Rick emerged from the back with a tray of coffee cups. They collected drinks, not wanting to break the somber silence. Jessie reached over to the speakerphone and dialed Ryan's cell.

"They knew exactly where to hit us," Cheryl said, voice just above a whisper. "Every single one of us."

"The symbols..." Jessie hugged herself. "Mine was a burning stage. They know what I do for the team."

"An old ukulele for me," Garrett added. "Broken in two and scorched."

Darwin opened his laptop but didn't turn it on, just stared at the lid. "We need to process two things. The attacks, yes. But also what I found about Val last night."

Aileen felt their eyes turn to her. Leader. Protector. The one who was supposed to have answers. Her fingers found the edge of the table, gripping until her knuckles went white. Morning sun streamed through the greenhouse glass, painting patterns on the floor that looked too much like the remains of her burning car. She closed her eyes and breathed slowly, once. Then again.

"They want us scared," she said into the waiting calm, surprised at how steady her voice sounded. "They want us to feel helpless. But look where we are."

She gestured around them. "We're at Bloomers. Together. They tried to isolate us, but instead..."

"We came home," Rick finished.

Aileen nodded, strength flowing back into her spine. "So let's use that. Darwin, show us what you found. Then we'll figure out who's really behind all this. Because whoever it is, they just made some mistakes."

"What mistakes?" Verona asked.

"First, they showed us they're afraid of what we might find. Of us." Aileen straightened up, releasing her death grip on the table. She ignored the muttered "they should be" from Cheryl.

"And second, they made me really, really angry…"

Ryan perched on the window seat, watching a police cruiser make a slow pass. The others clustered around Aileen's massive oak dining table, now covered with laptops, notebooks, and half-empty soda cans and coffee cups. A plate of Rick's special cookies sat mostly untouched in the center.

"Start with this morning," Darwin said, making notes on his laptop. "Gloriano shows up during the attacks. How did he know?"

"He said he 'saw them coming.'" Aileen pushed away from the table, pacing. "But coming from where? And why was he watching at all?"

"And why help?" Cheryl added. "He's not exactly team material."

Ryan turned from the window. "He helped me once. At the library, when some guys were hassling me. Just walked up, stood there until they left. Didn't say anything, didn't do anything. Just… existed in their space until they got uncomfortable."

"That tracks," Garrett said. "Remember when Darwin and I met him? Same thing. Quiet strength, not threats. He can be rattled, but it takes something pretty big."

Darwin chimed in. "Yeah, I was plenty scared at that meet. I thought he might go nuts, but all he could talk about was wedgies." He blushed while the others chuckled.

Jessie pulled up a database on her laptop screen. "His school records show a sharp drop in disciplinary issues last year. Almost like…"

"Like he's trying to change," Darwin finished, not disturbed by Jessie's encroachment on his computer-data demesne. "But change from what? To what?"

Darwin looked at the ceiling, his expression going faraway. "How old is he now?"

"Seventeen, last month."

Darwin nodded. "So he got a job, dollars to doughnuts. Sixteen, that's when that can happen, right?"

Aileen confirmed Darwin's deduction about age and employment.

Verona tapped a pencil against her notebook. "He knows Paco's gang. That's obvious from this morning. But he's not with them, not really. Paco's guys are all about showing off their connections."

"And showing up to help us isn't gang behavior either," Rick added, taking one of his own cookies.

Aileen stopped pacing. "So we have someone who knows the gang's moves but isn't part of them. Who helps but doesn't explain why. Who's trying to change but can't quite break free of his past." She looked around the table. "We need to talk to him."

"I'll go," Darwin said, volunteering immediately. "Garrett too. Right, buddy? He responded to us before."

Garrett nodded. "He's more likely to open up to us than adults. No offense."

"None taken," Aileen said. "But be careful. Whatever's going on with Gloriano, someone burned up my car this morning. We can't assume anything."

"We'll be careful," Darwin promised. "But Gloriano's either part of this or he isn't. And after this morning..." He glanced at his notes. "I think we need to know which."

Aileen picked up her handbag as a car approached her front curb. "I've got an appointment about insurance."

Ryan stood up as another police car crawled past. "Just remember what he did at the library. Sometimes just standing there is a message."

The team fell quiet, considering. Outside, a siren wailed in the distance, and Rick grabbed another cookie, eating to calm the stress.

"Find him," Aileen said. "Talk to him. But at the first sign of trouble..."

"We run," Garrett finished. "Fast."

"Me faster than you," Darwin said as he closed his laptop. "Time to see if our mysterious Latino wants to explain himself."

✧ ¤ ✧ ¤ ✧

The front door clicked shut behind Aileen, and the team's focus shifted in seconds.

"We need to talk about protecting her," Rick said, gathering empty cups. "Everything that's happened, the vandalism, the threats, my beating..." He paused. "It's all been aimed at Aileen."

Cheryl grabbed a roll of paper towels and some spray and started cleaning, needing to do something, anything.

"We all need protecting," Ryan protested. "You think I'm hiding here for my health?" That brought guffaws from the team. Ryan blushed hot pink.

Rick continued: "Look, Aileen's the real target. Bloomers? They hit her in her career, her livelihood. Maybe they thought she'd simply fold and leave. And her car, gone. Could have been her house." Ryan shuddered.

Verona looked up from her spot near the kitchen doorway. "But you were beaten," she said. "I saw what they did to you."

Rick winced as he tested his sore shoulder. "Yeah, but I was just in the way." Rick shrugged, hurting again. "They probably expected to find Aileen alone that night. I was a complication, not a target."

"Doesn't matter," Jessie cut in. "The point is, Aileen needs protection now. Real protection, not just us trying to watch everything at once. Couch has a few capable people, but with all the bedlam recently, I bet they're stretched thin."

Ryan straightened in her window seat, a small smile playing at her lips. "I know exactly who could help. Scruffy."

"Scruffy?" Jessie raised an eyebrow. "The homeless guy? And you can't exactly go find him yourself right now."

"I'll go," Rick said. "Ryan, how do I find him?"

"Piggly Wiggly. Just wait. He'll show up eventually. He always does. He'll see you before you see him."

The team dispersed shortly after, a police cruiser appearing for everyone except Rick. He watched them leave, then grabbed his light jacket off the hook; spring storms had been threatening all day. His phone showed three Ubers nearby.

114

As he waited for his ride, Rick mentally rehearsed what to tell Scruffy. How much would the old vagrant need to know? How much would he believe? How much could he really process? Finally, what could he really do? Ryan believed in him, but that couldn't be enough.

His jacket pocket crinkled as he fidgeted. He'd automatically stuffed a few dollars in there for emergencies.

His phone pinged. The Uber was two minutes away.

BE CAREFUL, Verona texted.

Rick smiled, typed back **Always**, and headed out to find a down-and-out man who might be their best chance at keeping Aileen safe.

Rick paced the cracked parking lot, trying to look casual while checking his phone. The Uber had dropped him twenty minutes ago. Faint shadows stretched across broken asphalt, and the wind carried a hint of rain. The neglected neighborhood preyed on his nerves, his senses, and he wished for eyes in the back of his head.

A rustle from behind the dumpster made him turn. Not Scruffy — just a plastic bag dancing in the breeze. His heart rate dropped a few beats. The empty store loomed behind him, its faded sign missing letters: PI LY WI GL .

"You Ryan's friend."

Rick spun. Scruffy stood there, a ghost materialized from nothing. Rick was so startled that his brain skipped. Did Scruffy have his own Star Trek transporter? How bizarre.

Scruffy's army jacket hung loose, but his eyes were sharp, alert. Rick felt he was being x-rayed to his very core, and that Scruffy now knew more about Rick than he did about himself.

"Yes, sir. I'm Rick."

"Don't sir me, kid. Never an officer. Ryan okay?"

"She's safe. But..." Rick hesitated. "She sent me. We need help. Someone's trying to hurt Miss Aileen."

Scruffy's weather-beaten face didn't change, but something shifted in his stance. He reached into his jacket, and Rick tensed. What emerged was tiny, white, and mewing. Dirty and hungry, and not more than four weeks old.

"Hold this," Scruffy ordered, depositing the kitten in Rick's hands. The creature was grubby and smelled of spoiled milk, but friendly, immediately purring against Rick's chest.

While Rick absorbed this development, Scruffy prowled the parking lot's perimeter, checking sight lines. His movements were precise, practiced. "Tell me," he said, standing ten feet away, his back mostly turned to Rick. Always scanning.

Rick explained everything. The car bombing, the symbols, the attacks. Through it all, Scruffy moved in gradually smaller circles, ending up back beside Rick.

"Bad business," he muttered. "Gonna need help. Got some buddies. Veterans. We look out for our own."

"Miss Aileen isn't —"

"She helps kids. Makes her one of ours." Scruffy's tone left no room for argument. "We'll watch. Day and night. Silent guard."

"How many —"

"Enough." Scruffy's eyes focused somewhere distant. "Some of us... We need purpose. Something worth doing." He looked at the kitten in Rick's arms. "You find that one a home, we got a deal."

Rick nodded, watching Scruffy, wishing his dad was anything like this odd man. "I will. I promise." He knew Bloomers didn't need a third cat. He'd figure it out. He stored the sleepy critter in a jacket pocket, tail first, and made sure it wouldn't fall out.

"Good." Scruffy turned to go, then paused. "Need supplies. Beer. Snacks. Nothing fancy. No MREs."

"I can —"

"Leave it by the dumpster. Different times. Don't get predictable. No MREs!" he repeated. His voice softened. "Tell Ryan... tell her we're on it. On watch."

Then he was gone, melting into the gathering darkness like he'd never been there. Only the purring kitten proved the encounter had happened at all.

Rick's phone buzzed: his Uber arriving. He checked the kitten. "Guess I've got two missions now, little one," he told it softly.

Thunder rolled in the distance as the first drops of rain splashed on the broken asphalt.

Chapter Twelve

Threatening spring weather heightened the tension in Aileen's rental car. Rick sat in the front seat, equipment list clutched tight, while Verona kept watch from the back seat. They made it exactly three blocks from Bloomers.

"Two guys on phones," Verona said suddenly. "Outside the coffee shop. Looking our way."

Rick's grip on the list tightened. "Mrs. B —"

"I see them." Aileen checked her mirrors. The morning traffic felt too light, too coordinated.

Two blocks later, orange construction barriers narrowed the street. A man in a safety vest waved them toward a detour, a second man leaning on a shovel.

"That's wrong," Rick said. "I didn't hear about any construction —"

Verona blurted out "Their clothes don't seem right —" when three motorcycles roared out of a side street.

Rick grabbed the wheel, yanking right. "Gun!"

The first bike went down, rider sprawling, his automatic pistol murdering some asphalt and a light pole. Verona screamed as the back window exploded, the shotgun blast peppering her with bits of glass as she rolled onto the floor. Aileen fought the unfamiliar car, hitting the brake instead of gas. The second bike clipped their bumper, spinning out.

The third rider raised his shotgun again. Aileen swerved up onto the curb. The second blast went wide. She jerked the car back onto the street, aiming for the other side and the third attacker. The rain-slick street caused the rental to slide, crossing into the path of the shooter.

He laid his bike over, losing the weapon and slamming into a fire hydrant.

Aileen found the accelerator. The rental car screeched forward, leaving chaos behind. In the rearview mirror, the "construction workers" were already gone.

"Everyone okay?" Aileen's voice shook. "Any blood?"

"Yes, fine," Verona confirmed. Rick nodded.

Rick unclenched his fingers from the equipment list, crumpled beyond recognition. "I think we need a new plan for getting computer gear."

A police siren wailed in the distance, too late as usual.

"Darwin can order online," Verona suggested weakly.

Aileen managed a long, shaky laugh and turned right on Azalea Street. "Good idea. Let's go home."

Darwin and Garrett asked around but got no real leads on where Gloriano might be. Maybe he went away somewhere. Wednesday wasn't supposed to be a holiday, but the district decided to use their "snow days" and give the schools the rest of the week off. Snow days, Darwin mused.

They found themselves in a part of town neither one had reason to venture into. They asked a friendly lady if there was some place where they could get a soda or something. "The Stand," was all she offered, and pointed. Garrett doffed his hat in thanks.

The duo spotted Gloriano exactly where they didn't expect him, stocking magazines at Cooper's Newsstand. He wore a clean white apron over jeans and a plain black t-shirt, arranging fishing magazines in perfect rows.

"No way," Garrett whispered.

Gloriano looked up, tensed for a moment, then slid the last magazine into place. "Give me a minute," he said, disappearing behind a rack of paperbacks.

Darwin glanced around the store. Ancient wooden shelves stretched to the ceiling, filled with newspapers, magazines, and books. The air smelled of paper and coffee from the small counter near the register. An elderly man, presumably Cooper, dozed in a worn armchair near the window, reading glasses perched on his forehead.

Gloriano emerged without the apron, a cigarette already going. "Outside," he said without heat, leading them through a side door into the alley. Stacks of bundled newspapers waited for recycling. A cat sunned itself on top of one pile.

"You work here?" Garrett couldn't contain the question.

"Two or three days a week, a few hours. Plus extra shifts when Mr. Cooper's arthritis acts up." Gloriano leaned against the wall, arms crossed. Not threatening; defensive. "That gonna be a problem?"

"No, it's..." Darwin searched for words. "Unexpected."

"Like me showing up that morning at Brannigan's?" A hint of challenge in his voice.

"Exactly like that." Darwin met his gaze without blinking. "How did you know about the attacks?"

Gloriano studied them both for a long moment. He crushed out his cigarette as he thought. "I hear things. Some good, some bad. Can't tell you more than that."

"Can't? Or won't?" Garrett asked.

"Both." Gloriano's shoulders tensed. "Look, I'm trying to... I want to…" He huffed. "There are things I can't change. Past stuff. But I can choose what I do now."

"Like warning people about gang attacks?" Darwin pressed.

"Like having a real job, '*Cito*," Gloriano retorted, gesturing at the newsstand. "Mr. Cooper gave me a chance. Nobody else would." He paused. "Well, almost nobody. Ryan's mom did once, at the library. I screwed that up. That's why I turned *Doña* Aileen down last summer."

Darwin and Garrett exchanged glances. This wasn't the conversation they'd expected.

"The gang," Darwin started. "Paco's people. Are you —"

"No, on my *abuela's tumba*." Gloriano's response was instant. He flashed a sly grin. "But they think I am. And that's..." He looked up at the drippy spring sky. "That's complicated."

121

Darwin tilted his head. "So you really know stuff," he said.

Gloriano waved him off, then stopped. He stared at Darwin like he was some predator's lunch. Squinting, Gloriano gave a tiny nod.

A bell tinkled inside the shop. "Glory?" Cooper's wavering voice called out. "Need you on these new arrivals."

"Coming, Mr. C!" Gloriano straightened up. "Look, I want to help. But there are things I can't tell you. People I can't..." He shook his head. "Just be careful. It's bigger than Paco's gang."

He turned to go, then stopped. "And don't tell anyone about this job. Please. It's the one normal thing I've got. Paco would gut me and laugh doing it if he knew."

The side door closed behind him with a soft click. Through the window, they watched him help Cooper unpack a box of books, handling each volume with careful respect.

"Well," Garrett said finally. "That was..."

"Yeah." Darwin pulled out his phone to text Aileen. "I think we just found out that Gloriano's trying to write a different story for himself."

"Question is," Garrett said, watching Gloriano shelve books, "will they let him?"

Later that afternoon the teens huddled around the dining table, laptops and notes spread everywhere. Cake crumbs decorated the table and documents in a random pattern, and the sink had a collection of soda cans.

"This is interesting," Jessie said, reading news on her phone. "There's a report that Marshall Boucheron died late Monday night or Tuesday morning." She set her phone down; it was almost dead.

"Not another murder?" Ryan asked. Jessie shrugged.

"He was already so sick," Rick said.

"Could be poison," Garrett offered.

"You and your poisons!" Cheryl said. Garrett shrugged.

"So Gloriano stocks magazines," Cheryl said, processing Darwin's report. "And helps old Mr. Cooper with his arthritis. How very, —" she trailed off.

"While somehow knowing gang movements," Garrett added. "But not being in the gang. He must be one sneaky guy."

"It fits," Ryan said from her window perch. "Remember the library? He helped my mom for a bit, but didn't want anyone to know. As soon as his secret got out, he quit."

Garrett spoke up: "He mentioned the library job. He said he screwed that up, though. And he said that was why he turned down Aileen's job last summer. Too public, Bloomers."

Darwin's fingers flew across his keyboard. "If we remove Gloriano from our suspect pool, and reconsider all our data..." He spun the laptop around. "Everything points to Trey."

Verona leaned in. "The timeline works. Access to Boucheron accounts is likely. The connection to Paco's gang definitely works, if we believe Rick." Rick responded with a quick pinch of Verona's arm, and Verona pretended to cry.

"And he's got motive," Jessie added. "If Val's innocent —"

A car door slammed outside.

"Aileen's back!" Rick hissed. "Places, everyone!"

The teens scrambled, transforming in an instant from a serious meeting to casual activities. Ryan and Rick jumped over the sofa and claimed the game console controls while Verona positioned herself for optimal heckling. Jessie grabbed her phone, Darwin wandered the living room studying family photos, and Garrett retrieved his guitar from its case. Cheryl snatched a cookbook from the kitchen.

Aileen's key turned in the lock.

She stood in the hallway, taking in the placid domestic scene. Rick button-mashing while Ryan dominated their game. Verona offering colorful commentary, mostly about Rick having four thumbs. Jessie apparently deep in conversation. Darwin studying pictures like he'd never seen them before. Garrett strumming random chords. Cheryl absorbed in... was that...?

"That cookbook is upside down," Aileen said flatly.

123

Cheryl looked up, clearly embarrassed.

"Jessie, your phone isn't even on." Jessie glanced at her dark phone. "Ah."

"Darwin, you haven't moved to a different picture this whole time."

He stepped back from the wall. "They're... very interesting?" He shrugged.

"Your guitar isn't tuned to your normal standards, Garrett."

He looked down at his travel Yamaha guitar. "I was... Just gonna fix that?"

Aileen crossed her arms. "Anyone want to try again? Or should I list more evidence of your collective guilt?"

The teens exchanged glances. Ryan put down her controller and the game scrolled on, revealing they'd been playing the same fifteen seconds on loop.

"We figured out who really killed Ethan," Darwin said finally.

"And it's not Gloriano," Rick added. "Wait until you hear how we know."

"It's Trey," they finished in unison.

Aileen sank into her favorite chair. "Tell me everything. And Cheryl? You can turn the cookbook right side up now."

The long, black Mercedes idled half a block from Aileen's house, its tinted windows and blinds guarding the occupant. The day's rains had gone, but the dark asphalt reflected streetlight. Trey drummed fingers on the steering wheel, watching teenagers filter out of the house. Police escorts appeared for most of them, Couch's one useful decision.

He recognized them all now. The computer geek, Darwin. That cowboy musician kid, Garrett, getting into his beater ride. The marksman girl. The blonde who worked at Lendon's. Each of them part of Aileen's smarmy little detective club. Each of them helping her get closer to the truth.

Ryan wasn't among them. She must be inside, hiding. Still alive.

Trey's fingers stopped drumming. The scar on his cheek twitched, a souvenir he'd collected during his own teenage years, a lesson from when he'd failed someone important. He touched it briefly, remembering the lesson. Sometimes pain was the only teacher people really understood.

He wanted Ryan to understand. Deeply. Permanently. Her pretty face would tell a story after he was done. A warning to anyone else thinking of walking away from his operation, from him.

His phone buzzed. Quentin. Just what he needed.

"You're supposed to be handling this," Quentin's voice dropped the temperature in the Mercedes ten degrees. "Instead, I'm hearing Aileen's bunch of babies is still investigating. Still causing problems."

"I'm working on it."

"Work faster. Or I'll remind you what happens to people who dissatisfy me."

The call ended. Trey's hand went to his scar again. He'd seen what happened to someone who disappointed Quentin. He'd had to bury one who disappointed Quentin twice.

Movement caught his eye. A shadow detached itself from the darkness, approaching his passenger side window. Trey reached in the center armrest for his pistol.

A tap on the glass. The town's homeless man, Scruffy, stood there, looking almost bored.

Trey opened the passenger window about three inches. "No money, go away," Trey said.

Scruffy's response was clear through the narrow gap. "Leave."

Something glinted in Scruffy's hand. Not asking, then. There were no percentages in wondering who could get off the first shot. Trey understood.

Trey put the Mercedes into gear, anger burning in his throat. As he pulled away, his rearview mirror showed more shadows moving in the darkness. How many were there?

His phone buzzed on vibrate against his thigh. Probably Quentin, demanding results again. Trey ignored it, his scar burning with remembered pain. He'd find another way to get to Ryan. To all of them.

125

The Mercedes disappeared into the night, leaving only questions in its wake. In the darkness, Scruffy's platoon watched in complete silence.

Chapter Thirteen

Morning light filtered through Bloomers' front windows, casting long shadows across the empty sales floor. Maundy Thursday crept through Silvergrove's streets, the town unnaturally still before Easter weekend's usual chaos. Rick welcomed the pause as it gave him time to work on several small tasks in the store before Aileen would show.

Rick finished checking the greenhouse, making sure everything was in order. Dew still clung to the outside plants, promising a moderate spring day. While restocking a display of seed packets, he heard the bell above the door. Early buyer, he thought.

Gloriano stood at the checkout counter, looking nothing like the street-tough kid they'd known before. Pressed slacks, a crisp button-down shirt, hair neatly combed. He looked like someone trying to prove something. Maybe looking for a job.

"Morning," Rick said, keeping his voice low and level. Warmth, but not too familiar.

"I want to talk," Gloriano said. "About everything."

Rick leaned against the counter. "Sounds serious." He burned with curiosity, not letting it show. 'Everything' could cover a lot of sins, from violence to drugs. Was he about to confess to participating in the attack on Aileen? Rick felt under the counter with his knee, checking that the cricket bat was still there.

"You need to go to Chief Couch with me." Gloriano's words tumbled out fast, like he'd rehearsed them. "Tell him everything I know."

Rick hesitated. "That's a big step."

"I know." Gloriano started pacing, hands moving as he talked. "But I can't... I can't keep doing this."

"I can go," Rick offered. "Make it easier. I'll go to the station right now, if you want."

Gloriano continued to walk through the display tables, touching everything, feeling nothing. "Man, I can't go there! Cops everywhere. Couch, maybe I can deal with him. Alone. At the stadium, maybe."

Gloriano stopped mid-pace. His eyes darted to the front window view where Miss Betty's ancient oak spread its branches. A figure stood in the deep morning shade, barely distinguishable.

"NO!" Gloriano's response was instant, visceral. He bolted for the back greenhouse exit, leaving the door swinging.

Rick rushed to the window. The shade shifted. Nothing. Nobody. Just the oak tree and morning shadows.

"Gloriano?" he called. Nothing.

Outside, a door slammed. Gloriano was gone.

Rick wondered: Was Gloriano saying no to going to Couch? Or something else entirely?

Aileen arrived early, sliding into a booth with a view of both doors. Two steaming coffee cups and a plate holding a kolache and croissant waited. The kolache was prune, of course. Couch's peculiar favorite.

She never understood the restaurant's name. Coffee and Margaritas? Who decided that combination made sense? Yet somehow, in Silvergrove, it worked. She'd never met Toad either; she doubted he existed.

Couch entered like a hungry bear emerging from hibernation: cautious, scanning, his police instincts never switched off. He nodded at Aileen, circled the room once, checking every corner before sitting.

"Coffee's hot," Aileen said. "Kolache too."

"Appreciate it." His grunt was almost a thank you. He took a massive bite, crumbs flying. For a moment, something like a smile flickered across his face. She couldn't remember him smiling, even when he knew he had Val dead to rights.

Which brought Aileen back to her purpose. "We've got new information about Val," Aileen began. "She's innocent."

The last bits of Couch's kolache paused partway to his mouth. "Another theory?"

"Not a theory. Proof." She outlined Darwin's ATM video evidence, watching Couch's expression harden, then soften, then harden again.

"You keep changing your story," he said.

"Because the truth keeps changing." Aileen matched his tone. "Darwin can show you the videos at the station. Multiple timestamps, multiple locations. Val couldn't have killed Ethan."

"Truth is truth." Couch gulped down the last of his brew.

"Facts are facts," Aileen countered. "Truth is what you make it out to be."

Couch opened his mouth to respond just as his radio crackled.

"Chief? Paco's gang spotted on Wisteria Street. Unit's requesting backup."

He stood in an instant, grabbing his hat and club. "We'll continue this later," he said, in a way that left Aileen wondering if he really would want to continue.

The door swung shut behind him. Aileen sat, surrounded by half-empty coffee cups and pastry crumbs.

"Later," she murmured, and signaled the waitress for a refill. And another pastry, just in case.

✧ ◻ ✧ ◻ ✧

Trey's Scotch caught the morning light, gold on amber. He'd been drinking since dawn, watching some mindless reality show, when Quentin's shadow filled the doorway.

"Drink?" Trey asked, already knowing the answer.

Quentin's look could have smothered the fires of Hades. Trey turned away from the bar.

"Your failures are mounting," Quentin began. Each word landed like a hammer. "Aileen Brannigan should be dead. Her team should be scattered. Instead, they're getting closer to the truth."

"Paco's gang —"

"Incompetent." Quentin's voice cut through Trey's excuse. "You were supposed to eliminate one blowsy, middle-aged gardener. One. And you can't manage that."

Trey's hand clenched around his Scotch glass. "I'll have Paco take you out first. Then I won't have to split 60% of the profits with an armchair strategist."

"An armchair strategist who keeps this operation running while you drink before noon." Quentin stepped closer. "I can run this gang without you. Keep all the money. All the connections."

Their dance of threats went on: each word a knife thrust, each pause loaded. Quentin smiled. Not pleasantly. Trey paused in wonder at the change.

"You have options," he said. "Leave town. If you can make it out alive." A pause. "Or die right here. Now."

Trey went still.

"Or," Quentin continued, "you can prove you're still worth me carrying. Kill Val. In the next 24 hours. Do that, and our... partnership remains."

The silence stretched between them. Outside, a bird sang, completely unaware of the darkness filling the room.

Andy Burrell gripped the steering wheel like he was piloting a spacecraft, not driving to a used car lot. Aileen watched him, barely containing her amusement.

"Nervous?" she asked.

"What? No." His knuckles went whiter.

"This isn't a date, you know," she said, letting just enough teasing come through.

Andy glanced over and realized she was playing him. He relaxed, smiling.

Hendricks Auto Sales sprawled across a sunny corner lot, rows of vehicles gleaming under the spring sky. Andy walked with her, offering opinions, but it was clear Aileen knew exactly what she wanted.

The blue Hyundai caught her eye immediately. Two years old, certified pre-owned, immaculate interior. "This one," she told the salesman.

Andy challenged her. "You sure? Why not that green Honda? It has more features."

Aileen smiled. "Nah, green's not my color. Blue is." She was already considering what name to give her new, blue friend. Garrett had his Angel, why shouldn't she name her car?

"And the Toyota?" Aileen shook her head. "Well, okay. You came here for a car. Let's go find the manager."

While paperwork churned, she chatted with Andy. "Friday morning delivery," the finance manager confirmed. "Unless you need it sooner?"

Andy's hopeful look made her laugh. "Friday's perfect."

The Drowsy Poet bookstore felt like sanctuary after the Hendricks showroom's fluorescent lights. Aromas of fresh espresso mingled with the earthy smell of paper. Aileen attacked the puzzle book section with the enthusiasm of an addict finding her fix. Crosswords, logic puzzles, cryptograms, sudoku: She gathered them in a growing stack.

"Withdrawal?" Andy asked.

"Severe," she confirmed. "What with all the excitement, I've completely burned through my stash at the store and at home."

Judge Davita Canton materialized between mystery and travel sections, elegant even in casual clothing. She and Andy exchanged pleasantries while Aileen continued her book gathering.

"How are those wonderful teens doing?" Davita asked. "I heard about the vandalism at Bloomers."

"Recovering," Aileen said. "Resilient bunch."

"And Gloriano?" The judge's question carried weight.

"Not really part of the group," Aileen answered after a moment. "But... in contact."

Davita's smile held complexity. "I had him in my court two years back. Good kid underneath. Economically challenged, but a solid family. Especially his uncle, as you know. I'm hoping he gets a real chance." She continued, "He's at that critical age. One more mistake could mean adult

131

court. And that..." Her voice trailed. "That would be the end of any hope."

Aileen's mind wandered back to Gloriano's sudden appearance as her car burned. She still had doubts, but Davita's thoughts carried real weight with her.

Aileen promised to check with her brigade to see what might be done.

At the register, puzzle books stacked high, she caught Andy's eye. Just friends. Just helping each other out. She tilted her head at the two stacks of volumes, and Andy took the hint.

The bell above the door jingled as they left, carrying possibilities.

Aileen asked Andy if she could buy him dinner as thanks for his help. He hesitated, she insisted. He agreed, feigning more resistance than his face showed. Then came the back-and-forth about what to eat and where. They agreed on pizza, fast and simple.

Paradise Pizza lived up to its name, if paradise included ear-splitting arcade sounds and children's jubilant chaos. Andy navigated the pandemonium like a seasoned captain, introducing Aileen to what must have been half of the middle school.

"Carlos, how's that science project coming?" A high-five. "Maria, I heard about your debate team win!" A proud smile.

Aileen watched, fascinated. These weren't just students to Andy. They were his kids. She now understood why school people loved their jobs.

The large combo pizza was indeed heavenly. Real, stringy cheese; a sauce that must have some secret ingredient that Aileen couldn't place; fresh red onion and yellow bell pepper; mushrooms on her half, black olives for Andy; pepperoni, mild Italian sausage, and Canadian bacon scattered all across. The portions were generous too. She told Andy it would be too much to eat, but at the end there weren't even crumbs.

Aileen wanted to know if Andy would like dessert. He patted his paunch and declined, explaining he'd had too many sweets this week. Maybe she knew of a good gym? They laughed, friends who understood.

After pizza and introductions to the middle school youth they returned to her house. Andy hesitated at her door, shy again. Aileen thanked him, dropped her massive stack of puzzle books on the antique console, which creaked in protest, and waved as he drove away.

Only after he turned the corner did she realize he'd wanted to kiss her. "Maybe," she thought, "I need dating advice from the teens." The dance happened too long ago for her, signals forgotten.

The evening was too beautiful to stay inside. Her front garden spaces needed attention, particularly with Easter only days away. She worried how it would look if the garden center's operator had wilted flowers. Not great advertising. Gloves, tools, hose. She attacked the neglected planters, losing herself in the rhythmic work of cultivation.

She didn't hear the motorcycle until it shut off in her driveway.

Paco relaxed on a Triumph that screamed expensive maintenance. Chrome gleamed. Paint looked fresh. This was no street gang bike; this was a man's prized possession.

"Afternoon," he said. Not a question.

Aileen kept gardening. Waited.

"My guys'll recover," Paco said. "Bikes too. They'll fix what they broke as punishment." He leaned forward. "I'm not mad, they knew the risks when they volunteered." He tilted his head, trying to make sense of Aileen's careful motions in the planters. "That's not why I'm here."

"Go on."

"Back off the investigations. Next time, we won't miss."

Aileen looked up. No fear. Just... curiosity. Had all the shocks dulled her emotions?

"Gloriano one of your people?" she asked.

Paco laughed. Not pleasantly. "Morning Glory? He's just a mascot. We're dropping him soon."

"Why?"

"Can't keep his mouth shut. If he doesn't learn, he'll regret it."

Aileen nodded. She understood the message perfectly.

Paco gave a wry salute, fired up his bike. The roar split the quiet evening. He sped off, and the whispering silence of evening settled over the neighborhood once again.

As the big bike disappeared, Aileen began to shake.

Just another Thursday in Silvergrove.

Chapter Fourteen

Dawn broke pale and thin over Silvergrove, the kind of light that promised nothing good. Dakota moved in the shadows, more habit than strategy now. Five days out of jail, sleeping in woods that ate further into his bones each night. He was down to pure survival instinct.

The back alleys told stories, tales that Silvergrove chose to ignore. He remembered some of the trails from his childhood, others from when he and Ethan had been part of the burglary ring. A torn fence, overgrown ivy hiding property lines. Drainage easements that were highways for predators and prey alike, overgrown with bushes. Garbage cans that hadn't been moved in weeks. Dakota knew how to read these marginal spaces; they were his map, his sanctuary. Changes in the area would sometimes fool him and he'd backtrack, always finding the correct path again.

He was closer to his goal now, the backside of that godforsaken garden center. Why did someone have to buy it, try to make it work? That guy Katsuda hadn't been able to make it work, years ago, and everybody said the Japanese were all great with plants. How could some no-name hag from who-knows-where think she should move in and try? It had sure put a kink in Dakota's plans: Wait until Ethan got out, dig up the loot, split it up and run. He'd even thought he would give Ethan the larger cut, since he took the fall for both of them. Only thing to do.

A police cruiser turned down Oak Street, slowly scanning yards. Dakota pressed himself against Mrs. Dinsdale's garage, breath tight in his chest. Close, too close. The cruiser's spotlight swept inches from where he stood, and he remembered every time he'd been caught, every time his luck had run out.

flashlight, glowing from the inside like it was alive. He'd sell the rest and keep the cat, he really would. Thinking of the art's beauty brought back the ugliness of that cursed night. An apparition from out of nowhere, yelling. Ethan's startled strike, the crooked fall, the horrible sound and smell. Dakota couldn't recall how they got out, or why Ethan had ended up with all the haul, but he didn't care then. Now, he cared.

One more look. Just one more. Then he'd figure something out. Half a loaf was better than starving, and he was so hungry, tired. So goddamn tired of running.

Bloomers' back fence looked the same. No secret markers. No hidden signs. Just weathered wood and trailing morning glory vines. Dakota's fingers traced the fence line, searching for something, anything, that might tell him where the loot was hidden. He dragged his shoes around all the big trees and got nothing. Couldn't be a little tree, not after seven years.

Nothing. Not a damned thing. Not even some nuts to eat.

The realization hit like a punch. He was done. Alone. Out of options.

Rick was placing trays of planter begonias when Gloriano slipped in through the back greenhouse door. Not sneaking, but definitely not announcing himself either.

"I heard something. I need to let somebody know. Let you know," spilled out of Gloriano like seeds out of a packet. "But if this gets out, no matter how, I'm dead." Gloriano couldn't stand still, pacing as far from the big glass windows as he could.

Rick kept sorting blossoms, giving Gloriano space. Casual, but attentive. "I'm listening. But you ran last time. Why now?"

"They've marked me, *hombre*. I think the gang has orders."

"Orders from who?"

"Trey. He thinks he's *vale*, some *jefe grande*." Gloriano's hands moved restlessly. "I just saw Paco getting orders from, well, you figure it out. Trey doesn't handle the money. The operations. Trey's just... a front."

"Why tell me?" Rick didn't look up from the seedlings. He struggled to keep his excitement from showing.

Gloriano laughed. "*Amigo*, I got connections. You got connections. I help you, you help me. You'll know who to tell." Gloriano stopped pacing. "Because..." He looked out the greenhouse window. "Because somebody's going to die. Somebody already has."

Rick's hands stopped moving in the dirt. "Ethan?"

Gloriano shook his head. "No, you got that all wrong. Somebody bigger."

Rick thought it over. "Marshall."

"*Bueno*, you're smart," Gloriano continued. "And that *malacopa perra* Val's next. I don't mean *mala pata*, bad luck." His switching between English and Spanish was giving Rick a headache.

Trey thinks he's making the calls, but he's only *pez pequeño*."

Rick tilted his head, questioning.

"Tiny fish, man." Gloriano fished around in a pocket, either nerves or he wanted a cigarette. A shadow passed outside the window. Gloriano went rigid.

"I shouldn't be here," he said.

And then he was gone again, leaving Rick with more questions than answers.

Another night of fractured sleep. Ryan's eyes burned, pupils scratching against eyelids like sandpaper. Three nights of half-dreams, half-nightmares. Trey's voice. His hands. The threat. Always the threat.

Three nights of frightened half-sleep at the Piggly Wiggly, guarded by that sweet goofball Scruffy. Ryan knew he was all right, you just had to look beyond his clothes and hygiene. He loved cats, he had to be a good man. She had taken a whole litter the strange man had found, once, though she had to give them to the shelter. One day her parents would let her keep a pet. For now, she knew someone who would share kits with her, when she asked. Enough.

She had thought the crazed replays at night would stop once she was safe. Aileen's house was a great hideaway, her bed was soft and her food was plentiful. That's when she learned that moving from Scruffy's unnerving space to luxury was no cure, no end to Trey's clammy hands on her, every night, over and over.

She rolled over, her phone's blue light painting wan shadows on the wall. 5:37 AM. Too early. Too late. Sunrise soon, though.

Sleep wouldn't come. Not anymore.

The shower was her first act of rebellion. Hot water washing away... what? Fear? Shame? She scrubbed harder than necessary, watching steam curl against bathroom tiles. Each movement deliberate. Each breath a small declaration. She felt guilty about all the hot water swirling away, but she couldn't stop.

Jeans, the dark blue ones. Comfortable, safe. A soft hoodie; gray, nondescript. Clothes that wouldn't draw attention. Clothes that could help her disappear.

Her hands shook slightly as she braided her hair. Muscle memory from martial arts training kept her fingers moving even as her mind churned. She knew how to fight. She knew how to escape. But escape wasn't enough anymore.

Something had shifted in the night. Between exhaustion and clarity, a decision formed. No more hiding. She had to exorcise the night demons or she'd be trapped the rest of her life. There had to be a way.

She stared at her phone, thumb hovering over the keyboard. Outside her window, Silvergrove was waking up: garbage trucks rumbling, early joggers padding down sidewalks, folks leaving for work. Another day in hiding unless she acted now.

Jessie's contact popped up. Ryan typed: **Will you help me get out of here?**

Instant response: **Yeah, you can come to my house, we'll have fun.**

Ryan sighed. Classic Jessie. Missed the point entirely. She needed more than a sleepover.

Another text: **Maybe later. I need something else.**

She scrolled to Rick's number. Hesitated. Then: **Help me get out of here.**

Rick's reply came immediately: **You having trouble with Aileen?**

No, not that. Her fingers sped across the keys. **I need to unlock this cage.**

You need to fight back.

138

How??? she typed.

Tell someone like Couch what happened to you.

Anger bubbled up, uninvited. Didn't Rick understand? She couldn't let this out into the open, the shame would end her.

Shame was just another prison, she realized. She would ignore it and anyone who wouldn't stand by her. Rick would understand, he had to, he'd fought his own shame after his beating. He'd conquered it, with friends.

Something clicked. A spark. No lifetime of fear, and not revenge. Justice.

Ryan heard Aileen downstairs, making coffee and puttering. Ryan's feet carried her to the kitchen before her brain caught up.

She sat in silence in the breakfast nook, not disturbing Aileen's routine. When her current savior looked over, she blurted: "I want to report Trey. To the police, to Couch."

Aileen put down the skillet and turned, patient. "For what, exactly?"

"He attacked me. Raped me."

Aileen moved slowly, sitting down before saying anything. "Ryan, *gra dom*, have you told your parents anything?"

Ryan couldn't look up. "Only that I'm sleeping over at Cheryl's and she's teaching me to shoot."

"Listen carefully, Ryan. Did he rape you?"

The direct question hung in the air. "No," Ryan confessed, breathing deeply. "But he could have. He grabbed me! He was going to."

"And he didn't because —"

"I kicked him. Hard. Maybe he'll never have kids." Ryan was too embarrassed to mention Trey's threat of kidnap and sale again.

Ryan could feel Aileen's anger, cold and slow as a glacier, as she considered what Ryan had just confessed. She stared down for long minutes, a

Aileen stood up, powered off the range and grabbed her bag. "Then we tell the truth. Only the truth."

Silvergrove Police Station buzzed with morning routine: phones ringing, officers shuffling paperwork, the smell of stale coffee hanging in the air. Delilah waved cheerily but didn't stop to visit.

Once in the Chief's office, Aileen closed the door. Sounds muted to a level that a shaky girl could handle.

Couch listened, his lined brown face growing more animated with each of Ryan's measured words. Threats. Drugs. Assault. The story emerged like a sketch being filled in, line by careful line.

Couch focused, scribbling notes throughout Ryan's account. No interruptions, only transcription.

When Ryan finished, Couch didn't just sit, he exploded.

"I've always wanted to nail that slimy bastard," he said, literally dancing between file cabinets. His boots scuffed the worn, checkered linoleum, toes tapping an impromptu victory jig. "Years. YEARS I've had him on my radar. Always playing me for a fool, hiding behind the Boucherons."

Aileen watched, bemused. Ryan looked shocked by the grown man's unfiltered enthusiasm.

Couch grabbed his gear — notebook, radio, jacket, hat, baton — in one sweeping motion. He suddenly remembered his pistol. He went to the bottom drawer of his file cabinet and took out the worn belt. "This is it. This is THE moment."

And then, without another word, he was gone, leaving Ryan and Aileen staring at the swinging door, Ryan's accusations hanging in the air like a just-freed bird.

Trey was going down.

The bevy of black-and-whites tore up the Boucheron drive like a pack of hunting hounds. Three cruisers, lights spinning, gravel spraying. The hunters howled down the half mile of trees. Couch drove in the lead, two additional units flanking.

The cruisers skidded into position in the inner courtyard. Couch and the two beat cops fanned out, weapons drawn. Professional. Practiced.

The massive garage doors stood open, sunlight glinting off polished chrome and expensive metal.

Couch grabbed the bullhorn. His voice boomed, unnecessarily loud: "TREY ANTONIO SPALDING! COME OUT NOW. SHOW YOUR HANDS!"

Inside the garage, Trey was mid-polish on the Rolls-Royce, a grand old crate that held more secrets than most humans. He froze, then ducked behind the car's gleaming fender.

"What the hell?" he yelled back. "What's this about?"

Couch fumbled with the bullhorn. The other police winced in anticipation. They sighed simultaneously when Couch put the horn down. "Assault complaint," Couch shouted. "Against a woman."

Trey's curse was immediate and visceral. "That damned girl!" He sat on the garage floor, his back to the classic's bumper, and swore he'd finish the job on her.

Trey thought hard, then an idea formed. A calculated relaxation spread across his features. The jail. Val. His task. Time was running out.

He raised his hands slowly, a performer's gesture of surrender. Walking into the yard, he saw the servants' faces pressed against the mansion windows. In the office window, a shadow figure: Quentin, he was certain.

Trey smiled. Waved.

The cuffs clicked shut, and Couch's victory dance began again.

Chapter Fifteen

The Lyft pulled up to the station. Rick and Gloriano stepped out into the morning's growing heat. Inside, Couch looked up from his desk, still riding high after Trey's arrest. His grin was pure predator: satisfied, triumphant.

"What've you got?" he asked before they'd even fully entered the room. Couch leaned back in his ancient desk chair, hands linked behind his balding head.

Gloriano's hands moved restlessly. "I hear you put the *picado* on Trey Antonio." A quizzical side-eye from Couch. "You arrested him."

"You damned right!" Couch almost yelled. "He's done."

Gloriano cleared his throat, looking to Rick. He continued: "Trey's operation isn't small. It's structured, and not his structure. Paco's gang. They're not doing random things. The attacks, they're targeted."

"How big? Targeted how?" Couch leaned forward, his demands like bullets.

Gloriano sighed. "Attacks on specific businesses. Protection rackets. Here and around the area. He's moved into drugs too. But someone's directing him. Trey gives orders, but..." Gloriano hesitated.

"But?" Couch prompted.

"Someone else is pulling bigger strings. I don't know who," Gloriano lied. Okay, not exactly a lie, he rationalized. He was pretty sure, not certain. "But Trey's not the top. He's just *el puente*." At Couch's blank stare: "The bridge, the guy in the middle."

Couch looked at Rick. "Why does he keep doing that?"

Rick wanted to smile, but with Gloriano watching he chose his best serious look. "Chief, his English and Spanish are both excellent. When he uses a Spanish phrase, he's actually more on target." Rick did smile

143

then. "I wish I knew another language as well as this man here," and he reached across to give a supportive shoulder-squeeze.

Couch nodded. "Drugs?" Couch asked.

Gloriano breathed in, then nodded. "He's got mules and dealers at the high school."

Rick watched, silent. Gloriano was revealing just enough to keep Couch interested, a careful dance of information.

Gloriano continued: "Moves them through the manor. One of the Boucheron cars has a hide so Trey can transport. Using gangsters like Paco's crew. To collect."

Couch nodded as Gloriano connected old information with new. He pushed the phone's intercom. "Delilah, bring me that file on assaults on teens from a year ago." He switched off.

"Anything else?"

Gloriano asked for water and Delilah brought a bottle when she dropped off the file. He settled in to complete his expiation. Or his doom. He pressed on with his tale. Rick watched in wonder.

The jigsaw was filling in, but the puzzle's picture remained just out of focus.

✧   ¤   ✧   ¤   ✧

Aileen's Whataburger Spicy Chicken Sandwich sat half-eaten, growing cold while her mind raced through the evidence. Rick watched her, recognizing the look of someone solving a complex riddle.

"Gloriano gave Couch a lot," she said, more to herself than to Rick. "But not everything."

Rick nodded. "He's holding something back. Carefully."

"How do you see Gloriano's performance for Couch?"

Rick bought a moment by dipping a French fry in mayo, then chewing. He swallowed and leaned in. "He's good, ma'am. Maybe the toughest one of us all. I say he's in with us. He's scared too, so he's cagey. Wouldn't you be?" he challenged.

Aileen remembered her sandwich. "Yeah," she squeezed out around a mouthful. "Yeah, you're right. You really think he's with us?"

Rick nodded. "I'd stand back-to-back with him against all of Paco's rabble." A long pause. "So where next with all this?"

Aileen grinned and snitched one of Rick's fries, forcing him to cover with both hands.

"We're running out of bad guys, eh?"

"Thank heavens!" Rick said.

"We keep putting Marshall on the list, then taking him off. Now he's dead," Aileen said in low, even tones. "If he was the top, then who's looking to step into his shoes? And did they kill him?"

Rick nodded at all the unanswered points. "Trey, maybe," he tried.

"Trey's arrested. He's not the end, I think." Aileen took a mechanical bite of sandwich, chewed without tasting.

"Quentin?" Rick suggested.

"Absolutely on the list," Aileen said. "Though he's just a butler. He doesn't ever leave the Manor, really. So how does he do it? What are his connections? What are the mechanisms?"

"He'd have access to Marshall. But why now." Rick pulled his fries closer, one hand making a wall between him and his boss while he ate, thinking.

They batted theories back and forth. Val's name surfaced again.

"She's a victim," Aileen stated. "Not a mastermind. Look at the ATM videos. Look at her dates with Kyle."

Rick considered. The town's whispers aligned with Aileen's assessment. Val was chasing good times, not running a criminal enterprise. He smiled as he chewed his last fry. "Can't use the Kyle dates, though. We blew up his last one, remember."

Aileen tried out a tired smile. "Yeah, and that didn't work. Val's in jail because of us. she belongs there, I think. Just not for murder."

"Couch has the linchpin," Rick said. "Trey."

"For now," Aileen murmured. "God, I hope you're right. This could end our troubles, put Silvergrove back right again."

Rick agreed, then added: "Or makes things worse, if somebody tries to get Trey out of jail by force. Or Paco's army goes nuts." He shivered at the remembered attack on the way to Diva's. They were shooting to kill.

Aileen's smile inverted. She stood up, ready to leave.

Rick cleared their table, gathering trash while Aileen refilled her coffee. A ritual of thinking, processing.

As they prepared to part — Rick back to Bloomers, Aileen to go to the house so the repair guy could fix her broken window — the quiet holiday afternoon hummed with unresolved tension.

The jail cell's single fluorescent light flickered, casting harsh shadows across the floor from Val's frantic movements. She paced like a wounded animal, alcohol withdrawal making her motions erratic, desperate.

"DRINK!" she screamed at the solid metal door. She shook the bars of her cage. Nothing. No response.

Trey watched, calculating. Delilah's last cell-check had been minutes ago. No cameras. No witnesses. He couldn't have set this up better if he had tried.

He approached the bars between their cells, casually strolling. Almost friendly, not the usual professional deference he showed her. "Need a drink?"

Val lunged forward, eyes wild. "Oh God yes, save me Trey, like you always do!"

"Snuck in a flask," he said. "Over by the wash basin. Your favorite when it hurts. Vodka."

Her desperation made her rush to the corner by the wash basin. She pressed her face against the bars, trembling. Trey bent over, pretending to search, to fumble.

Trey exploded upward, cobra-quick. His hands shot through the bars, fingers clamping around her throat. One strong, practiced twist. A moment of resistance. Then nothing. He held her until she was soft, unmoving.

He bashed her head twice against the corner of the basin in her cell. He dropped Val to the floor with a muted thump.

Her body crumpled. Perfect.

Trey lay back on his bunk. Delilah would be by soon on her rounds. Everything looked... normal.

Val's body lay face-up on the cold, hard floor of her cell. The Medical Examiner's forensics tech, James Levenson, had closed her eyes but touched nothing else. The crime scene photographer had come and gone.

James stood back and scanned. Yeah, it's possible, he thought. He heard she had a big drinking habit, and at the time of death she was likely shaking from withdrawal. He had seen plenty in his decade working at the Silver County Morgue. It made sense.

James turned to his case waiting on the bed, opened the top and side, and grabbed some sample swabs. He felt this one was a no-brainer, but he'd go through the whole process, step by step. He got paid the same either way, and the ME could be a total pain about skipped steps and how that messed up his reports. By the book, he drilled, by the book.

First some swabs on the washstand stain, then a parallel swab on the woman's damaged temple. He logged them by number and location. What next?

James got down on all fours and looked carefully all around. He spoke his observations into his recorder, like always. Nothing out of place, really. Though what was that on her neck, dirt?

Delilah came in with fresh brew. James indicated she could place his cup on the back of the wash basin, where the soap should be. Even the ME wouldn't complain about that, he thought. The Old Man had his own caffeine habit, he would have done the same.

One more sample stick, rubbed on the light blue spot on Val's neck. That's odd, nothing came up. The stain looked the same. He logged the stick anyway, then leaned in, tilting his head for a better view.

"Find something?" the somber jailer asked. James looked around at Delilah. She was usually the most cheerful person in the whole police station, but now she frowned, worried.

"There's a stain on her neck. Doesn't wash off. Did the photographer capture that?" he asked. Delilah shrugged. "I can get the station's camera," she said. James waved her off. He snapped a photo with his phone. Acceptable, with that new app that marked the photo with an unchangeable date-time-location stamp. He pocketed the phone.

James reached out to move Val's nose a bit, looking for more stain. Her head fell over, startling James. That's odd. Couldn't be a broken neck, could it?

James sat back into a squat, hands on his thighs. "Delilah, get the Chief." His level tone urged her to hustle.

Chief Coach practically ran into the cell. "What?" he demanded.

"Chief," he said, pointing to Val, "her neck's broken." He tilted Val's head, revealing the neck's unnatural angle, "Broken cervical vertebrae, technically speaking."

"So what? She fell."

"That's just it, Chief. The head wound could have killed her. The broken neck, sure. But we don't ever find both injuries in simple falls. If this is an accident, I'll eat your hat."

"Official?" Couch demanded.

James shook his head. "I'm not the examiner or the coroner, sir. I still stand by my off the record statement, though."

Delilah shifted her weight back and forth. She'd been the last one on duty, the last one to check Val's cell. Her hands vibrated against her uniform slacks.

Levenson's gloved finger traced the bruising. "See these marks? I thought they were stains. They're fingertip impressions. She was grabbed, hard. Not strangled but restrained."

Couch leaned in, professional distance momentarily forgotten. "Could she have fallen... awkwardly?"

Levenson snorted. "Not a chance. These injuries are deliberate. Someone grabbed her. Twisted. Hard and fast."

Delilah whispered, "But how? The cells..."

Couch's eyes narrowed. He knew exactly who had access to the cells.

"I don't want her, but I need Aileen Brannigan," he muttered, reaching for his phone.

Ryan and Aileen were sharing tales about school. Aileen had fresh caffeine potion so she was feeling mellow. Ryan was stirring tiny marshmallows around in her lukewarm chocolate. Aileen was pleased to see Ryan's natural buoyancy returning after their tense morning at the station.

Their phones chirped simultaneously. Ryan's screen filled first:

BREAKING: VAL BOUCHERON DEAD IN JAIL CELL

Local Rich Woman Found Murdered

Rick: **You seeing this?**

Jessie: **OMG WTF**

Darwin: **No WAY**

Aileen's incoming texts were more professional:

Couch: **I'll call soon. I may want you.**

Rick: **This is BAD!!**

Ryan's initial reaction was pure, savage joy. A visible shiver of satisfaction ran through her body. "He's dead," she whispered. "Trey's going down." She got up from the table and danced all around the kitchen, singing some modern nonsense that Aileen couldn't follow.

Aileen interrupted. "Hold on. Why are you so sure?"

Ryan's triumph faltered. Her eyes narrowed. "Someone killed Val. In a locked cell. Next to Trey."

"Exactly," Aileen said. "So who could do that?"

They exchanged a look. The possibilities were terrifying. Ryan sat back down and gulped her drink. "Inside job?" she asked.

Aileen could only shrug. "Motive?"

Ryan's confidence returned. "Payoff. There's too much money around that family."

Aileen paused. "So, who would do that? Val had the money. That would be the most bizarre suicide in history."

Ryan deflated. Couldn't she see it? Trey was right there. He had served Val for years, though. Could he do it? And why? She thought for minutes before continuing.

"Not just Trey," Ryan said. "Someone who can move through locked spaces. Someone with power."

"Bingo," Aileen nodded. "Someone who could make a murder look like... nothing."

The room grew cold. Their earlier confidence about Trey being the kingpin now felt paper-thin.

When Couch's call came, Aileen grabbed her jacket. Ryan, small and scared, locked every door and window. She retreated upstairs, pulling blankets around herself.

This killer could be anywhere, go anywhere.

Chapter Sixteen

Levenson crouched in Val's cell, Couch and Delilah hovering behind him. Trey watched from the adjacent cell, silent and tense. Aileen was on her knees, not touching any evidence, close enough to see.

"These marks," Levenson said, pointing to Val's neck, "aren't from a fall. Deliberate strangulation, or some such. She was grabbed for sure."

Aileen raised an eyebrow, asking for permission to touch. She shuddered inside, but her new courage stood with her. She squeezed an ear, moving the head gently. "Why isn't there any rigor?" she asked.

Levenson considered her point. "Well, I'm not the ME, but I bet he'll say the broken neck won't get very rigid, even if the rest of the body does." He reached over and moved a thumb, showing that rigor mortis was showing up.

Aileen stood up. "Chief, I've got to ask. Who has keys to the cells?"

Couch looked at Delilah, his frown ordering her to take the question.

Delilah shuffled back and forth a bit. "I just did my rounds. Everything was normal." She caught herself. "I have one set, there's a common set in the locker, and there's the special backup at City Hall, just in case."

"Anyone go to the keys locker?" Aileen asked. Then just as quickly: "Forget that. You couldn't possibly know, it's a common area. People go there all the time, you likely wouldn't even notice. Or remember."

Couch's eyes narrowed. "How long between your checks?"

"One hour. Standard procedure, you know that. I can show you the logs."

Couch relaxed. Aileen realized he didn't suspect his jailer. She was more like a second daughter than a police officer, to him.

151

"What else is there?" Aileen asked Levenson.

Levenson traced the bruising, now more pronounced as time passed. "Big hands. Strong. I'd say from the size, male. Fingertip impressions suggest a deliberate grip."

He tilted Val's head, revealing the unnatural neck angle once again. "Broken cervical vertebrae. Inconsistent with accidental injury. Not if the head wound did her in."

Couch glanced at Delilah. "Who else was here? Any other staff?"

"Just me. And Jake, he manned the front desk at the time."

Aileen watched out of the corner of her eye. She noticed Trey holding motionless in his cell. Sweat beaded on his forehead.

"Someone entered this cell," Aileen said, stepping forward. "Impossible. But they did it."

Levenson nodded. "Murder. No question in my mind. Of course the ME and the coroner will have the official say."

✧ ⌑ ✧ ⌑ ✧

Good Friday's dusk crept into Aileen's breakfast nook where she sat trying to make sense of what she'd seen in Val's cell. The pieces refused to fit together. Her cell phone's sharp ring scattered her thoughts.

"Is Ryan there?" Maylene Ruggle's voice carried an edge. Aileen called Ryan to the breakfast nook. Ryan appeared in the doorway, then slid into the chair across from Aileen. Aileen put the phone on speaker between them, catching Rick's slight head-turn from his video game in the living room.

"I just talked to Cheryl's mom," Maylene continued. "You haven't been there all week? We need you home for Easter preparations, young lady, and I want to know where you've been."

Ryan stared at the phone, silent.

"Tell her," Aileen said. "Couch already knows."

Ryan's fingers twisted in her lap. "Mom, I... I was attacked on Monday. Some guys jumped me near the park." Her voice quavered. "I've been staying at Aileen's because I was scared."

"What?" Maylene's shock crackled through the speaker. "I'm coming to get you right now."

Ryan shot Aileen a panicked look. Aileen shrugged; this was Ryan's call to make.

"Mom, please don't." Ryan leaned toward the phone. "I'm okay now, really. I'll come home tomorrow, I promise. I just... I need one more night to process everything."

The silence stretched. After a long pause, Maylene sighed. "Are you sure you're all right? Did they hurt you? Do you need anything? Clothes? Your Easter dress?"

"No, I've got everything." Relief softened Ryan's voice. "Thanks, Mom."

After Aileen ended the call, Rick materialized in the doorway. "When are you going to tell them about the drugs?"

"Soon." Ryan wouldn't meet his eyes. "Just... not yet. I can't handle that conversation right now."

"You should go on home," Rick said. "I mean, I like having you around, but Trey's in jail. The danger's over."

Ryan shook her head. "My parents mean well, but they're not great listeners. I need space to think."

Rick studied her for a moment, then grinned. "Want to think while I destroy you at Mario Kart?"

"Oh, please." Ryan pushed back from the table, energy returning to her voice. "I'm going to crush you. I need to work off some stress."

Rick caught Aileen's eye, throwing her a wink as they headed for the living room. "You can try, but it's not happening."

Aileen watched them go, the evening's shadows deepening around her. One crisis averted, but how many secrets could Silvergrove hold before they all came spilling out?

The jail settled into its evening quiet. Only echoes remained in Val's cell; evidence catalogued, surfaces sanitized, waiting for its next occupant. Trey slid from his bunk to the cold floor, his mind spinning. Val, dead in a locked cell. Right next to him. Quentin would know.

Each passing minute felt like a noose tightening. Quentin would sell him out. Paco's gang would be instructed to handle him. Inside or outside the jail, it didn't matter. Dead man walking.

When Delilah made her next rounds, Trey was a mess. Tears streamed down his face. His voice cracked.

"I need to see Couch. Now. Right now."

Delilah looked skeptical. "He's gone home." She wished her shift was over too, but she was doubling up. It was tough being the one jailer in town.

"Then get him!" Trey's voice rose, bordering on hysteria. "I can't wait. I have to talk to him. NOW!"

Delilah took a step back from Trey's vehemence. "Maybe Saturday," Delilah said. "Look, it's a holiday weekend. Maybe Monday."

Trey collapsed onto the cell floor, body shaking with sobs. "I gotta see Couch now. I gotta see Couch now. I gotta see Couch now..."

His plea echoed through the quiet jail, a man who knew his hourglass had run out of sand.

The mansion's library window glowed, a dim yellow smolder. Dakota tossed pebbles, precise and rhythmic, until a shadow moved behind the curtain.

Quentin appeared, silhouetted. "Who the hell —"

Dakota waved, an absurd gesture of casual invitation.

Minutes later Quentin led him not into the mansion, but across the grounds to Trey's garage apartment. Neutral territory. Smart, Dakota thought.

The apartment smelled of old leather and expensive Scotch. Quentin poured two fingers into crystal tumblers, pushing one toward Dakota. A small salute with his glass from Dakota, an unmoving stare from Quentin.

The bargaining began. "You've got exactly three minutes," Quentin said. "And that's generous."

Dakota's hands shook as he lifted the glass again. "The red jade cat. All the missing art and artifacts. It's my ticket. I know you want it."

Quentin's eyes narrowed. He knew how many millions that art assortment was worth. "I'm listening."

"Seven years ago, Trey knew something. About the treasure. I want my cut. You want... whatever you want." Dakota's desperation leaked through every word. He gulped Scotch, feeling it burn to the bottom.

"My cut?" Quentin laughed, short and harsh. "You have nothing. Absolutely nothing." His eyes kept the pressure on. He didn't sip the drink by his elbow.

Dakota slid an old, dilapidated photograph across the table. "This was Ethan's. He shared it with me. I don't know what it means."

Something flickered in Quentin's eyes. He made a decision. "One thousand cash. Keys to a car," Quentin said. "More generous than you deserve. Tell me exactly where."

"I can't," Dakota whispered. He knew he was tapped out; the end. The moment fractured. Dakota's drink splashed toward Quentin's face. Quentin, trained in the vicious streets of Dublin, blocked and struck. Dakota crumpled.

While Dakota lay unconscious, a plan crystallized in Quentin's mind. Fast. Brutal. Clever. Only Trey could lose.

✧　♯　✧　♯　✧

Afterward, Quentin wiped the blade, then wrapped it with a cloth. He'd take it, dispose of it, leaving no clues. Dakota's blood made a small, precise arc across the apartment's expensive Afghan rug.

He considered his escape. The mansion held enough valuables to fund years abroad. Jewelry. Artwork. Cash. Silver. Quentin chuckled at the thought of stealing the silver, something he hadn't done since he was a lad in Dublin, learning his trade.

The red jade cat? Irrelevant now. It would never be found anyway.

Tomorrow, pack. Drive. Gone. Then someplace warm, with willing wenches wearing next to nothing. Someplace with as little Silvergrove in it as possible.

Silvergrove would be a worn-out memory, nothing more.

155

Chapter Seventeen

The morning air pressed against the back porch like a warm, damp cloth. Aileen's sudoku grid waited, a complex mathematical challenge set aside the evening before. Wicked tough, she thought. This puzzle's a lot like the mysteries in Silvergrove.

Ryan appeared with a tray: steaming coffee in Aileen's favorite ceramic mug, biscuits golden and smelling of fresh butter, and small dishes of homemade strawberry jam and honey beside them. "Thought you might need fuel," she said, setting the tray down.

Aileen split a biscuit, spread it with jam, and looked up. "Ryan, I want to talk about Quentin. What do you really think about him?"

Ryan's fork paused in its rapid motions. "I barely ever saw the butler. Only Trey."

"I'm thinking that Quentin's more than a butler. Way more. Like maybe a murderer."

Ryan rejected Aileen's option. "It's Trey. Has to be. After what he had the gang do to you, after Ethan —"

"Stop," Aileen said softly. "Your anger is clouding your judgment. Trey's involved, yes. But he's not the mastermind. Think about the timing. The connections."

They reviewed what they knew: Quentin's mysterious background, working for Marshall Boucheron, the peculiar way information seemed to flow around him. The inconsistencies in the original story and action lines. Gloriano's observations. The deaths at the Manor.

Ryan went silent, her young face serious. The quiet stretched, filled with unspoken thoughts. Biscuits disappeared, slathered with butter and toppings. Aileen wanted more coffee, but wasn't going to break the moment to get some.

Aileen picked up her pencil. "Back to my puzzle," she murmured. Ryan watched a cardinal dancing in the bushes in a way that said she really wasn't watching.

Aha! Breakthrough. Just as the final number clicked into place, a moment of pure mathematical satisfaction, something else clicked in her mind. It really could be Quentin. Had to be. The pieces of the murder puzzle suddenly aligned with the same precision as her sudoku solution.

Precision wasn't proof. This wasn't some square of numbers in a magazine. "Last suspect standing" was a rookie mistake, and she wasn't a rookie at puzzles. She refused to be a rookie at solving murders. She needed data, though. Hard evidence. How to get that?

Ryan's phone chirped. "I should take this," she said, turning toward the house.

Aileen barely noticed, her mind racing. How to prove Quentin was more than just convenient? How...

✧ ¤ ✧ ¤ ✧

The hand-written sign on Bloomers' door announced "Holy Saturday Hours: 10 AM to 1 PM. Last Chance for the Best Easter Flowers!"

Chaos and efficiency reigned in a skewed balance in the front space. Rick hauled potted plants from the back greenhouse, one big flat at a time. Ryan sorted his offerings into the holes in inventory with mechanical precision. Jessie helped customers load purchases while Verona distributed Easter tea rose boutonnieres: crisp red for men, pristine white for women.

The shop hummed with pre-Easter energy. Cheryl and Aileen managed the point-of-sale, a dance of transactions and flower arrangements. They never bumped into each other while they boxed, bagged, and collected payments.

Near lunch, the rush to help customers slowed. The front area had only a few customers left, wandering around and touching the beautiful blooms. The teen girls gathered in the break room. Aileen stepped in for a soda, thanking them for their hard work. "You girls are like foster daughters," she said offhandedly.

Cheryl, unable to resist, asked about Mavourneen.

Aileen felt her shoulders tighten. "She's fine. School's going well."

"Is she coming to see you this weekend?" Cheryl continued, not reading Aileen's posture.

A customer's urgent call rescued Aileen from further explanation.

The teens exchanged glances. "She should know they don't get along since the divorce," Ryan muttered.

Cheryl blushed, then pushed back. "I didn't know they had problems. Hey, I didn't even know Aileen's divorced." She sank back, crossed her arms, and pouted; Jessie blew her a kiss.

Darwin and Garrett appeared with Gloriano in tow, walking quietly through the back entrance of the greenhouse. Gloriano looked both nervous and determined. Rick's welcoming arm settled Gloriano's obvious discomfort. All three young men sat, reaching for snacks.

"Tell us what you know," Rick invited.

Gloriano spoke quietly, describing what he'd witnessed while up at the manor with Paco's gang. The power dynamics were clear: Quentin controlled everything. Trey was muscle, not mastermind. Small corrections, subtle redirections; Gloriano had watched Quentin manipulate every situation. Many wouldn't have noticed, but Gloriano's street-trained observation skills caught the hints, the whispers. The change in directions from Trey, mid-order.

"Quentin's the real problem, *amigos*," Gloriano said. "Trey's just following orders."

Aileen, catching a break between frantic flower shoppers, listened intently. The pieces were falling into place.

Outside, the first thunderclap announced the incoming storm. "It's closing time," Aileen told the teens. "Get home before it gets worse."

Ryan yelled at Rick that she wanted lunch. Rick shrugged.

"Okay if I take Ryan to Sombrero Roja? I need my Tex-Mex fix." Aileen waved her assent as she hurried to shut down the store. She was so distracted by her chores and the rush to beat the rain that she didn't see Ryan and Rick hide in the storeroom. Aileen ran out the door, locked up, and sprinted the few yards to her blue Hyundai while huge drops splattered everywhere.

✧ ✕ ✧ ✕ ✧

"How long will we have to wait?" Ryan asked.

Rick hid with Ryan behind a large stack of potting mix bags. They both had their phones out, neither typing. Rick shrugged.

"Five minutes, tops. I think the rain will keep her from coming back, unless she forgot her purse. Again."

Ryan nodded, then looked at the weather map on her phone. "Ugly for the next several hours."

Rick finished a text, then hit send.

"The others will be back in five minutes or so. The two Ubers they're in, they have them circling out west a few blocks. No way Aileen sees them, even if she goes for groceries. I bet she goes straight home in this mess," he finished.

Ryan rolled her shoulders, trying to find a comfortable position against the lumpy bags of soil.

"Do you have some cash? I'm tapped out," Rick said.

Ryan squinted at him. "Why?"

"We have to pay the two rides. I know the other kiddos won't have enough."

Ryan nodded, a frown of distaste on her face. "It's drug money," she said.

"Okay. You can't give it back. This way, you're using it for some good, at least."

"I was going to leave it at the pet shelter."

Rick stood. "Good. But let's get our friends paid up when they return."

"It's time?"

"Yeah. I'll go check. You go on into the break room and set up. Leave the lights off, just in case."

Ryan stood and dusted off her slacks. "Right. We really need to figure this out, Rick." She handed him a pair of 20s.

Rick tilted his head back and forth, then moved into the front sales area, slowly, to watch for the return of the rest of Aileen's irregulars.

Quentin's fingers traced the delicate curves of a small bronze statue, wrapping it meticulously in tissue before placing it in another box. Six containers already filled, two rooms yet to be stripped. The computer files were stored on drives, carefully hidden in the Mercedes. He'd leave the computer. It was too big to worry about, too easy to replace. The art was important.

Each piece received careful examination. Original oils caught his eye; not just as valuable objects, but as memories of past conquests. His mind drifted, totting up murders like an accountant working a long ledger. Dublin. Marshall's assignments. Over a dozen, easy. Probably more.

"Beatings were always more satisfying than quick kills," he muttered to himself, a distant smile playing across his lips. Ordering others to do the dirty work, then sitting back to savor the details. Better than direct involvement. Control was the real pleasure.

The trafficking ring in Dublin. Now that had been a profitable enterprise. He regretted that loss, but he'd done all right in the States. Marshall never caught on to his diversion of money over the years. That old fool had had too much money anyway. Marshall was gone now, in the best way possible, and nobody knew what really happened but himself. Such delight.

Thunder cracked outside, earlier than expected. Quentin rushed to the back door, already too late. The courtyard was already a rapidly filling swimming pool.

"Damn," he muttered. "Should have moved the Mercedes." No matter. He had no need to suffer in the driving Texas rain. Once the storm broke he'd bring the car around to the portico. Plenty of time. No rush.

He returned to his methodical looting and packing, tissue rustling, boxes stacking neatly in the foyer. Another memory. Another treasure. Another escape planned. He smiled.

Chapter Eighteen

Saturday afternoon rain drummed against Aileen's windows, the continuing storm painting her garden in silvery sheets. The rain would perk up all of Silvergrove's gardens so they could glorify the coming Easter morning. Aileen mused about her part in that panorama and smiled.

She sat in her breakfast nook, a cold, sweating bottled lemonade beside her, replacing her arm bandage with a waterproof cover. A small grin, more determination than humor, crossed her face. She hoped she wouldn't get wet today, but just in case. She moved her arm from the shoulder, strong motions to test the fit of the new bandage. Perfect.

Puttering with small tasks couldn't keep her mind from returning to the problem she had to solve. Confronting Quentin. Easy to decide. Harder to execute.

Someone has to take this monster out. Not the kids. Never the kids. They'd earned their reprieve, their leisurely lunch or wherever the day would take them. They couldn't know. If they knew, they'd try to stop her. They hadn't earned the risks she was about to grasp.

Her mind raced through potential strategies. A gun? Laughable. She'd be more likely to shoot herself than Quentin. Cheryl's shotguns were beautiful and accurate, in Cheryl's hands. Not hers. She gave a short laugh at the image of her trying to sneak a shotgun up close to Quentin. So absurd. He was evil, not negligent.

No. Her only weapons would be words. Carefully chosen. Precisely aimed. She would make him submit, confess.

The trap at Casa Sol haunted her. So perfectly planned and executed. They had put Val in that cell, an innocent woman, and now she was dead. Murdered because of their misguided plan. The electronic surveillance had worked too well. Shame burned through her, a scalding internal tide.

"All my fault," she whispered. No blame to share with her teens. She swallowed it all.

She stood, washing her hands in a symbolic gesture of cleansing. No more guilt. No more hesitation.

What she needed now was a recorder. A microphone. Evidence.

He'd done it, Rick thought. He'd fooled Aileen. The team could now plan in peace. He texted the group chat: "Back to Bloomers. Now."

Nobody had gone far. They knew they needed to talk, to work out how to keep Aileen safe.

Rick moved back to the door, peering out, not assuming that Aileen had really gone. He made sure the lights stayed off and the Closed sign showed prominently, then he unlatched the door. Two Ubers swung by in order, disgorging teens who sprinted out of the rain. Each one looked somber, worried. Ryan waited in the doorway of the break room, touching each team member as they passed through. Comfort, acknowledgement, inclusion. Within ten minutes, the group had assembled, a wet, bedraggled cadre, electric with anticipation.

The group's energy splashed about like the Texas storm raging outside. Rick let the initial chaos run wild. Teenage voices overlapped, theories colliding. He banged a metal coffee cup on the breakroom table.

"This session of Brannigan's Battalion is called to order!"

A chorus of boos erupted. Paper clips and crumpled notes flew. The name game began in earnest.

"Aileen's Angels!" from Garrett. Immediate, thunderous booing.

"Aileen's Allies!" Two tentative votes and a shouted "better!" The others continued the detritus bombardment.

"Aileen's Marines!"

Darwin objected. "I hate water," he declared, to general laughter.

Gloriano watched, bewildered. How could they possibly accomplish anything with such pandemonium? After a moment. he remembered their previous meeting and nodded to himself. Somehow, this worked.

More names flew. More were rejected. The energy was pure teenage strategy session: part serious investigation, part pure joy.

Rick banged his cup again and leaned forward. "I asked you all back because I think Aileen's got a dangerous plan." Heads nodded. He ran the discussion around the table, Darwin recording every wild speculation.

"She's leaving town."

"She's going after Trey."

"She's visiting Mav."

Ideas flew. Rick squashed early objections. "Aileen wouldn't allow those just yet," he said. "We'll make the list and then we'll judge."

Gloriano remained silent until Rick pressed him. "Come on, you know more about how bad things can happen than the rest of us combined."

Gloriano grumped at Rick's portrayal, then accepted. He spoke in soft, accented tones. "She's going after *el Primer*, after Quentin. Must be."

Darwin moved that idea to the top of the list, striking the others. The room turned deathly quiet.

"When?" Rick asked. More silence. All eyes turned to Gloriano.

He fiddled with an unlit cigarette, then tossed it expertly into the trash. He chuffed, digging out his pack of smokes. He tossed them into the can as well. "Tonight, *mis queridos amigos*. Tonight."

He explained how precarious he thought Quentin's position now was. His employers dead, his top minion in jail. If he was still in the mansion he'd escape tonight, using the storm as cover. Deep consideration and gentle nods floated around the table.

"How do we stop her?" they argued.

Gloriano laughed. "Stop that stubborn *mujer*? Impossible."

Verona suggested protection. "Cheryl? She's the one with guns."
Cheryl popped up, ready to start now. Then she sat. "Wait, we're not
going to use a gun to make Aileen stop, are we? That's just wrong."

Gloriano waved at Cheryl, acknowledging her intelligence.

Ryan's eyes lit up. "Wait, guys! We've already got the perfect group.
We just need to find them in this storm."

Darwin's phone rang, startling the team. He patched the sound
through to his open computer, speaker ready. It was Aileen. "Are you
home?"

Crossed fingers showed all around. Darwin lied. "Yes. Why? Do you
need me back at Bloomers?"

"Can you do me a favor?" Her voice was quiet and small, a child
about to ask for the cookie she knew she shouldn't have.

"Yeah, sure. What do you need?"

"Darwin, honey, do you still have those electronic toys we used
when we ran the con on Val?"

"Yep. Right here in my computer bag. I never got around to putting
them away."

"I'd like to have one." No explanation, no enlightenment. A flat
request. The crossed fingers were vibrating.

"No problem. Ten minutes?" Aileen thanked him and abruptly cut
off.

Garrett started to drag Darwin away to Angel. The whole team
blocked him. "Lyft or Uber," Rick said. "I've already hailed one. Two
minutes out." He waved his phone.

Darwin grabbed his backpack, rescuing the Bosco, the orange tabby,
before shoving his computer in. "No need to stop at home. I've got
exactly what she needs."

Rick clapped his hand, the sharp crack grabbing attention. "Okay,
the rest of you, let's get going. You know what we need to do."

Outside, the early afternoon light brightened as the storm passed on.

Darwin arrived at Aileen's door, backpack slung over one shoulder, a wizard on a mission.

"The first storms have passed," he announced, stepping inside and checking out through the window. A few residual droplets hung from tree branches, the world washed clean and waiting. The sky wasn't clearing, though; more storms were forecast about dark and on into the night.

"Thanks for helping, Darwin."

Darwin opened his pack and started rummaging. "No problem, Mrs. B. I hope I brought the right ones."

Aileen raised an eyebrow. "What all did you bring?" She still couldn't believe Darwin lugged that big bag around every day.

Darwin pulled out a collection of miniature recording devices, "We've got about three hours before the next wave hits. Bigger storms coming around sundown, I hear."

He spread the devices on her kitchen table. Tiny. Detailed. Each one looked like it could hide in plain sight: a button, a pen cap, the edge of a picture frame. One looked like a brooch, nothing big or gaudy.

"Professional grade?" Aileen asked.

Darwin's grin was pure teenage certainty. "You kidding? Better than professional. These are custom. Some came to me modified, and then I changed some more stuff on them. I can activate them remotely, they've got encrypted transmission, and they'll record even if someone tries to jam the signal."

"Wait, they transmit?" Aileen said, deflating.

Darwin connected her face with her wishes. "Oh, they don't have to. They can keep the record on the box. Here, this tiny piece." He pointed at the back of one of the earrings. They were too big, clearly not her style. He had so many, though, she felt sure he'd have a perfect recorder. But she didn't want Darwin listening in.

"I think you'll like this one," he said, holding out a ring. "Goes completely unnoticed. This is just the mic, the recorder fits in this little flat pack, and that can go anywhere in your clothes. I could even style it into your hair."

The kid was showing off, but Aileen recognized genuine skill when she saw it.

"As for transmitting, you can leave the base unit up to a mile away and the transmitter sends there as well as keeps a copy."

In a matter of a few minutes Aileen had her setup. Darwin showed how easy it was to turn off and on.

"Can't it just stay on?" Aileen asked. Fumbling around on her blouse was not what she had in mind when talking with Quentin.

"Oh sure, but the battery's only good for a dozen hours or so. Yours is fully charged." He checked that the unit was running.

"I'm all set, I guess," Aileen said.

Casually, too casually, he added, "So. What exactly are you doing this for?"

Aileen's response came a touch too quickly. "I'm going to a meeting. With Andy and Couch. About Trey. I thought this might be better than taking notes. Less distracting."

Darwin's did his best to hide his skepticism. He hoped it was enough. He wished he was an actor, like Jessie.

She was going to do it, she really was. Darwin had to get back to the team.

✧ ⌂ ✧ ⌂ ✧

The sky darkened in the northwest, visible against the last strains of dusk, heavy with incoming storms. Aileen parked at the base of Boucheron Manor's drive, walking in even, purposeful strides. She hoped the blue Hyundai was hidden enough. She had a paring knife in her coat pocket, the biggest she could hide without it showing. She wore her black workout clothes, the looser set, and her like-new running shoes. She wasn't even sure why she had the blade. Her first defense, her only defense, would be speed.

Lightning flashed in the distance, still too far away to be heard. She went over her plan, such as it was, to get Quentin to talk. Her first assumption was that he wouldn't be afraid of a middle-aged gardener. That wasn't too far a stretch, if he really was a hardened criminal. If he was just a butler then she had nothing to worry about.

Her next assumption was the tricky one: That Quentin would want to talk, would want her to see his brilliance, his capability. All she had to do was provoke him, hurt his ego to start the flow. She thought she knew enough to taunt him with hints that she knew about his dealings. Let his ego spill out a confession.

She hoped she wouldn't have to insult him. She had no idea what a master criminal might consider an insult. You missed me? Your lap dog's in jail? Nothing seemed harsh enough to anger Quentin.

Aileen walked up the final bit of the drive. She saw Quentin loading a box of something into the Boucheron's Mercedes, under the portico. She called his name, clear but not very loudly. He raised his head, then smiled. Aileen waved like she wanted to borrow a cup of sugar.

"You lost?" he asks, pretending innocence. "Car trouble?"

"Quentin, I know," she said, a simple statement of fact. She stopped far enough away to give her options, though close enough that her recorder would catch everything. Including the thunder that was approaching at alarming speed.

"Oh lady, you're as ignorant as the day you were born." He opened the driver's door and leaned on it.

Aileen swallowed, then began: "Val. Ethan. Trey. Paco." Each name with a couple of seconds between. Slow artillery shells that Aileen could only hope would find their target.

Quentin's face went dark, affectless. "You have a few of the pieces, it seems."

"I have them all," Aileen taunted. "What can you give me to not talk?"

"You came for money?" Quentin asked with a smirk. "How uninspired."

"The world is full of mercenaries," Aileen said. "Some are just better than you."

"Better than me?" he spat. Quentin began reciting his criminal history like he was telling a child's story. Murders. Mutilations. Trafficking. A litany of calculated violence. Ireland, Texas, other places where Marshall needed to make something happen.

169

Horrified, Aileen struggled to maintain her composure. She asked clarifying questions or tossed in more barbs, ensuring Darwin's recorder captured every damning detail.

Leaning into the Mercedes' driver door, Quentin continued his monologue. Elated by her success, Aileen failed to read the danger.

"And now?" she asked. "Plans?"

Quentin's chuckle turned into something deep, monstrous. "My dear lady, I always have plans. Sadly, though, I must bid you a fond farewell. Forever."

Quentin jumped into the Mercedes, starting the engine. He flattened the accelerator and the excellent piece of German engineering didn't pause at all. The unmoving car became a massive weapon.

Tires screeched on the portico floor. Lightning illuminated the estate as rain began to pour.

Aileen yelled against the thunder. She turned and ran for the outbuildings, hoping to find a place to hide. She started across the open courtyard, sprinting flat out, faster than ever in her life.

It wasn't enough. Quentin circled, cutting her off, forcing her to turn and turn again. The Mercedes slung gravel everywhere. Aileen could hear Quentin's maniacal laughs. He hunted her like a black leopard after a monkey.

She couldn't breathe, slowing, failing. One last try, she grunted. Win or die. That big poplar. She screamed and sprinted, hope pleading against certainty.

Quentin swung the big German auto around and accelerated.

Aileen realized she wouldn't make it, she couldn't. She turned to face her fate, courage overwhelming resignation.

A gunshot. A second. The Mercedes' windshield starred, then shattered. Quentin whipped the wheel over, choosing flight over murder.

A dark figure appeared beside Aileen. Familiar. Gritty.

Scruffy.

He fired two more shots at the retreating car, then pocketed his weapon. "Rear tires gone," he said to himself.

Aileen hugged him so hard he lost all his breath. She released after a long moment.

"The car," Scruffy advised. "Don't run straight away. That's silly TV bull. Run at an angle. That's how you survive." Then he smiled, the biggest smile Aileen had ever seen him make.

Aileen turned at the sound of more gunshots, down the drive where the Mercedes fled. The car swerved back and forth, then rammed a tree, hard. The hood crumpled upward as the driver's door flew open. Quentin fell out into the mud, wounded, screaming. He was quickly surrounded by several more dark figures.

Sirens howled in the distance, rapidly approaching. Late as usual, Aileen thought, and she began to laugh hysterically in the pouring rain. She and Scruffy ambled down to the accident: One bedraggled matron cackling occasionally, and one silent, troubled man. Silvergrove's odd couple, out for a stroll. Along the way, smaller figures moved into the driveway lights, surrounding her. Her team, her victorious teens.

The cops arrived just as the menagerie reached the smoking Mercedes full of evidence.

The rain slacked off, storms drifting southeast. Near the wrecked Mercedes, an unlikely congregation gathered: Chief Couch, Aileen wrapped in a blanket, Scruffy and the teens. Scruffy's army had melted away like fog in sunshine.

Police technicians transferred boxes in choreographed moves from the Mercedes to a waiting van. Delilah's camera captured every moment.

Gloriano and Scruffy looked wary in Couch's presence. Rick's hand gripped Gloriano's upper arm, part support, part restraint. Ryan maintained a side-hug with Scruffy, silently proving solidarity.

Darwin recovered the recorder and handed it to Delilah for bagging. "I'll swear an affidavit Monday," Aileen said. Darwin would be there too. The entire team chimed in their commitment.

"So what did Quentin say?" Couch asked.

Aileen, wet, tired, and dropping off an adrenaline jag, still looked carefully at her kids. Verona caught her reluctance and said, "Oh come on, Mrs. B! We're big kids now!" Ryan reached over with a palm out; offering, begging.

Aileen stood up as straight as her aching muscles would allow. "Okay, but when this gives you nightmares, don't come crying to Mama Brannigan!" She turned to Couch, serious once again.

Aileen recapped the brutal narrative that Quentin had recited: murders, beatings, drugs, human trafficking. Couch nodded. "These we can verify."

The youngsters processed the monologue in silence. When Aileen ran out of words, they asked what they should do next. They agreed to meet at Bloomers after Easter church, not too early, not too late, and talk.

Stress and shock overwhelmed Aileen. She swayed.

"I'll drive," Rick offered.

Couch raised an eyebrow. "You have a license?"

Rick's smile was pure mischief. "Ask me no questions and I'll tell you no lies."

Couch muttered, "Officially, I didn't hear that," and returned to the evidence collection efforts.

Ryan put her arm around Aileen's shoulder and started slowly walking. "You realize we're never going to let you out of our sight," she lectured. "It's for your own good! I mean, just look at what stupid things you do when we leave you unsupervised!" Rick and Ryan exchanged a knowing look.

Aileen's weak sniggers punctuated their walk to the car as Ryan continued to play the angry adult. Scruffy watched them go from the deep cover of an evergreen, then was gone.

Chapter Nineteen

Easter morning's soft light filtered through rain-washed trees. Rick took an unexpected call from his mom, asking if he would join her and his dad for sunrise services. The kitchen was so quiet that Aileen could hear both sides of the conversation. Rick pitched a quizzical eye at Aileen, who countered with two pointed index fingers: your call, not mine. He dressed quickly and left for the outdoor Methodist services, leaving Aileen and Ryan on the back porch.

Aileen prayed that her strong right-hand man could begin to reconnect with his folks and find peace at home. It was a start, she hoped.

Steaming cups in hand, they sat in a silence that felt more like a conversation. The spring morning breathed with renewal; clean, fresh, hopeful. Birds sailed through the air in their springtime dance of pairing, filling the sky with natural hymns.

Ryan waited. Patient. Watching.

Aileen, cradling her cup in both hands, broke the silence. "Are you okay?"

"No, I'm NOT okay!" Ryan's response burst out. She caught herself and sipped her cocoa. The heat dissolved into pure disappointment. "What you did was incredibly dangerous and stupid. And you turned your back on us."

Aileen looked up, letting vulnerability show on her face. "Yeah, okay. Maybe I wasn't thinking clearly. But I didn't turn my back on all of you. I had to protect you. It was my call, my duty."

"So you knew it was dangerous!" Ryan sat up straighter. "That you could die."

A smile; tired, knowing. "Dangerous, I agree. I fooled myself. I let my need to expose Quentin make me forget my mortality." She shrugged. "Even old folks can make mistakes."

Ryan didn't gloat, didn't press. Instead, she pleaded: "Please don't ever do that again."

Aileen gave Ryan a mischievous grin. She reached out. Pinkie swear.

They dissolved into long, relieved laughter.

"I'm going to get ready for church," Aileen announced. "Coming with me?"

Ryan's response came instantly. "Someone has to make sure you're not unsupervised."

More chuckles as they headed inside to change.

Easter Sunday afternoon was warm, and the humidity made the air feel like luxurious velvet. There was just that hint, that promise, that the Texas summer wasn't far away. Aileen had just finished cleaning up after a light lunch. Church had been beautiful, especially meaningful after the past two weeks' tumult.

Ryan headed upstairs, hoping for a quick post-lunch nap.

The distinctive thrum of a powerful motorcycle announced Paco's arrival before he turned into the driveway. One rider. Alone.

Aileen wiped her hands and stepped outside. She nodded a cordial welcome, waiting.

"We're off," he said without preamble.

"Any place in particular?"

A shrug. "West. Or maybe Mexico. Me and the *compadres*. Looking for new opportunities." The Boucherons were finished. Silvergrove held nothing more for the gang.

Aileen offered a silent, unseen prayer.

"We won't be back," Paco added. "You and your *dragones feroces* would make trouble."

Aileen's grin turned feral. Her heart rate surged, not in fear but in victory.

Paco fired up his bike, gave an ironic salute, and rode away. Neighbors peered from behind curtains, watching the departure.

Easter Sunday, mid-afternoon, Brannigan's Bloomers felt like a singular sanctuary. With no customers, no helpers, this was a fine place to meditate, Aileen thought. She was glad she'd come early and given herself time to reflect and breathe. The heady aroma of the flowers that remained after the Easter sales rush filled every part of the store with nature's finest perfumes.

The three kittens played their learning games, battling each other, strafing and jumping, often two against one. Aileen had no intention of keeping them. Certainly not all three. Maybe just the orange tom, he was such a love bug when she worked at her desk. She watched them while contemplating.

The team drifted into the breakroom, leaving the front lights off and the "Closed" sign up. No shoppers today.

Aileen sipped an Adagio tea, Andy's gift, finding it surprisingly refreshing. The room filled with a subdued energy. No sadness. No happiness either. No clear emotion, except perhaps satisfaction.

She tapped the table with her pen. "I'm guessing you have questions."

The discussion unfolded in ordered steps. Quentin. Ethan. Val. Dakota.

Aileen chose her words with care, framing each revelation as their collective victory. This was their story as much as hers, maybe more.

Quentin had killed Ethan while Trey held him upright. Trey moved the body to the cemetery. Val's murder? Pure Trey, but under Quentin's direct order. Dakota's death, Quentin claimed self-defense. The coroner would have the final word.

Marshall and Ursula remained mysteries. Quentin's mysterious comments about the older Boucheron pair left gaps. With Ethan and Dakota dead, some truths might never emerge.

The treasure? Another unknown. The Red Jade Cat almost certainly wasn't in those seized boxes. More missing art remained out there, waiting.

Silence settled. Deep thoughts churned.

Darwin broke the quiet. "So Bloomers is fixed now? What's next?"

Aileen appreciated the pivot. "Bloomers needs minor repairs. Something I can work on when sales are slow. The New Bloomers is already better, thanks to the you all. Particularly Rick."

Rick blushed as the team cheered. Garrett suggested getting the blanket out of Angel's trunk and tossing Rick to celebrate. Heck maybe he could touch the glass at the top of the greenhouse!

Aileen's brutal silence was more than enough veto. They settled down.

"So, you mentioned plans for your business?" Verona prompted. Aileen noted that she was sitting close enough to Rick that they really didn't need two chairs.

"Maybe I'll have ideas tomorrow," Aileen said. "At the Ice Cream Social."

The teens erupted in song and dance, ready to party.

Chapter Twenty

Precisely at four, Garrett's Angel arrived at Bloomers, the automotive equivalent of a geriatric patient in need of oxygen. Five teens burst out: Garrett with his best guitar, Cheryl carrying a huge cake, Jessie and Verona wrestling an ice chest of mystery, and Darwin clutching cupcakes. Ryan and Rick had arrived earlier.

Aileen wondered aloud about Gloriano's absence. Moments later, he strolled confidently through the back greenhouse, an enigmatic wooden box in his hands. All she could see was dark, rich wood grain.

The break room turned into mission control. Paper plates and plastic utensils. Bottled drinks all around. Cheryl's cake centered on their 'war room' table like a strategic battle map, ready to show the way to delight. Darwin arranged cupcakes with scientific precision. Jessie and Verona scooped up various flavors of Blue Bell Ice Cream. Ryan, in full-blown manic phase, skipped around the room, peppering everyone with confetti and glitter.

The party was on.

Conversation flowed through the shop like water in a stream. Gossip, soccer finals (the Koalas were in, Rick was out), summer plans. Aileen captured their attention briefly, announcing a new greenhouse project near the back fence. Teen labor would clear the space, and there would be paid work through the summer. Wild cheers erupted.

Gloriano requested silence. Standing before Aileen, his beautiful old wooden box in hand, he offered a profound apology for his earlier resistance to her job offer, and for any of his behavior she might have found lacking. "Please accept this as a token of my sincere request for your forgiveness."

Aileen, flustered for the first time the teens had ever witnessed, gently took the box and thanked him.

She admired the unmarked box first. Maple or cherry, darkened with the passing years. She opened the box. Oh my, she thought, eyes wide. Artfully arranged inside, rested a collection of exquisite Easter-themed chocolate confections, each centered on their own pastel paper cup. Gloriano said he had crafted these himself, with help from his *Tío* and *Tía*. He bowed deeply. Applause thundered.

All the youngsters gathered around to admire the edible art. Rick attempted to snitch one with a tiny, pink bunny on top, and got a solid slap on his hand and a glare from Aileen. While she was distracted, Verona plucked out one with a cherry painted on top. Aileen turned just in time to see Verona nibbling and smiling. Rick signaled a thumbs up and ran over to get some before Verona could eat it all. Everybody laughed, and Aileen closed the box with a sharp snap before others could steal any of her extraordinary treats.

"Shame on you!" Aileen played in mock anger. "I'll leave a few for you all. Maybe. If you're very good."

Gloriano spoke up again: "Uhh, *Doña*, Brannigan, one small request, if I may. Could I have the box back when you're done? *Tía* Rosa uses it to hold thread and thimbles." The laughter was as loud as the previous applause. Gloriano's ears glowed red, but he smiled. He could take this. From his *compadres*, he could take it.

The evening dissolved into community celebration. Andy was fed cake and ice cream against his will, or so he claimed. Chief Couch grabbed a quick scoop of vanilla before static-filled talk on his radio pulled him away. Locals dropped in, checking on their favorite gardener and her young crew. Three energetic fluffballs had to be rescued often from doing damage to flowers or getting trapped in boxes. Ryan laughed when she found the white kitten face-down in her ice cream.

Darwin, cake threatening his keyboard with crumb warfare, displayed a news release on his computer: "Silvergrove Gardener and Teens Break Crime Ring." A paragraph detailed incoming funds recovered from criminal enterprises, enough to restore City Park and launch teen support programs.

He turned the screen for everyone to read, then returned to his ice cream.

Third helping.

✧ ¤ ✧ ¤ ✧

The party slowed naturally, the way good parties do: laughter softening into conversation, conversation softening into the comfortable silences of people who didn't need to fill them. Aileen sat with a fresh mug of tea, watching Ryan with the white kitten. The orange tom sat with Aileen. She had quietly decided to keep him, though she hadn't said so out loud yet.

"He's claimed you," Ryan observed, watching the kitten knead Aileen's lap. "You know that, right?"

"Bosco," Aileen said. "I'm calling him Bosco."

"After the syrup?"

"After my granddaddy's dog. He used to fall asleep right where Bosco's box rests."

Ryan tilted her head. "I'm picking this white one. If you'll let me."

"Your mom will skin you."

"My mom owes me one." Ryan was already smiling. "And she always wanted a Persian. This one looks Persian if you squint and don't look too hard."

Aileen laughed quietly, the kind of laugh she hadn't had in weeks. The third kitten, the calico, had attached herself to Cheryl, who was pretending to read on but kept stealing sidelong glances at the warm bundle curled into her shoulder. Three kittens. Three homes. Aileen would have to thank Scruffy.

Garrett picked up his guitar without announcement and started something gentle. Not a song, exactly, but the place a song begins, chord finding chord like footprints in fresh snow. Verona drifted to the doorway and leaned against the jamb, listening. Darwin closed his laptop without comment. Even Rick, who'd been on his fourth cupcake and showed no sign of slowing, set the cupcake down.

"I want to say something," Aileen said, and the room found a way to be quieter.

She looked at each of them in turn: Rick, Darwin, Verona, Cheryl, Jessie, Garrett, Ryan, Gloriano. Eight faces, eight stories. Three weeks ago she could have named only four of them.

"I'm not going to make a speech. I'm too tired for speeches and you're too full of cake." A small, expected laugh. "I just want you to know that I see you. All of you. What you did this month was not a small thing, and I won't pretend it was. You walked into something dangerous because someone you cared about was in trouble, and you didn't walk back out until it was finished. That is not a teenage thing to do. That is a grown-up thing, done by people who happen to be teenagers, which is harder."

She drew a breath. The orange kitten purred against her ribs.

"I don't have words for what you mean to me. But I have flowers, and I have a back garden with a lot of empty fence line, and starting in June, I'm going to need every single one of you. Paid work. Real wages. I already cleared it with Patrick at Northside."

A small storm of grins around the room.

"And one more thing. There are names we haven't said tonight, and I think we should. Marshall. Ursula. Ethan. Val. Dakota. Five people who can't be in this room. We didn't kill them, and we didn't fail them. But they're part of this story, and I don't want to forget them just because tonight is sweet." She paused. "Some of what we found isn't done yet. The red jade cat is still out there. And the name Cartwright. Quentin said it twice, and he meant it once."

"Cartwright?" Rick said.

"Don't worry about it tonight," Aileen said. "Worry about it after Easter dinner, when the dishes are done."

"After dishes," Verona agreed solemnly. "And after I sleep for two days."

Outside, the first stars were settling into the indigo sky over Silvergrove. Andy waved goodbye from the parking lot — he had Easter Vigil to get to. Chief Couch had long since vanished into another small-town emergency. The shop's grow lights warmed the greenhouse to a soft green glow, and the smell of damp soil and Easter lilies drifted out through the propped door, mingling with the sweetness of buttercream and the faint, distant sound of Garrett's guitar.

Aileen carried Bosco inside and set him in the orchid crate behind her desk. He yawned at her with absolute trust, curled into a tight orange comma, and was asleep before she finished smoothing the rags around him.

She turned off the front lights. Not all of them; enough to call the day done.

Tomorrow there would be the real, slow work of putting Silvergrove back together. There would be calls to make and reports to give and a Brannigan's Bloomers to keep open through whatever came next.

Tonight, there was cake, and there were kittens, and there was a guitar in the next room, and there was a place where her teens were laughing about something she couldn't quite hear.

Tonight, that was enough.

The End of

"Secrets of Silvergrove"

Books by Mitchell R. White

Brannigan Mysteries
Secrets of Silvergrove
Forget-Me-Nots and Forgotten Graves
Blue Iris, Blood Morning
Lotus, Lilies, and Last Courses (Summer 2026)
Roses are Red, Violets are Murder (Fall 2026)

Summers Rose Investigations
End in a Dead Heat
So Easy It's Criminal
Tacos, Sunsets, and Murder
The Drowned Duck (Summer 2026)

Writing as M. R. "Doc" White, Ph.D.
Samarqand: Prelude
Samarqand
Redeeming Lost Pegasus (Spring 2026)
Bloodwine Warriors Trilogy (2026)

Writing as Mitchell R. White, Ph.D.
The British Slang Handbook

ABOUT THE AUTHOR

Dr. Mitchell R. White, Ph.D.

Mitch White writes murder mysteries, cozy and otherwise, as well as science fiction and fantasy novels. His works can be read via the Kindle platform (tablets and computers), and soon will be available in print form.

Mitch White grew up reading the greats of his time in science fiction, fantasy, action and mystery. These stories encouraged Mitch to try his hand at writing while in graduate school, where he was fortunate enough to take creative writing courses led by Orson Scott Card. The demands of school and family prevented Mitch from publishing, though the "writer's bug" never left his soul.

Working through school found Mitch in roles from ditch-digging to nuclear non-destructive testing, mixologist to prep cook for a dorm of 1,200 students. All these experiences provided incentive to finish a doctorate in chemistry, with other degrees gathered along the way.

A rewarding career in science and technology, and a gratifying family life, left little time to write until retirement appeared on the horizon. Traveling the world as a consultant scientist and engineer provided exposure to and appreciation of many cultures. Nothing broadens one's perspective quite like travel, and Mitch's experiences in other lands informs his interests and prose.

Mitch also taught as visiting professor in the sciences at several universities. He provided technical training in semiconductor and computer manufacturing, process optimization, quality improvement, and statistics to over 20,000 attendees on five continents.

Avocations pursued through the years include cooking, mixology, chess, travel, photography, fostering Golden Retrievers, and recreational computing.

Somewhere in all this chaos, Mitch found time for family, raising a daughter and now spoiling a granddaughter.

During retirement, Mitch performs as a professional musician when not writing. Mitch finds that the two avocations cooperate well, and he looks forward to years of fun, creative endeavors.

He lives in the suburbs of Austin, Texas, very close to the center of the universe.